To Nico

Peter Coffey

HEE HAW

HEE HAW

PETER CAFFREY

HEE HAW

ISBN: 9798862440645

Acknowledgements
Thanks go to Mike Rankin, Leeanne Wright, Lindsay Crook, Corrine Morse and Christina Pfeiffer for their help and support.

OTHER BOOKS BY PETER CAFFREY

The God of Wanking

Dog Food

Peter Caffrey's Fucked-Up Bedtime Stories (Series One)

The Butcher's Other Daughter

Whores Versus Sex Robots (And Other Sordid Tales of
Erotic Automatons)

Dolls' House Diabolic

The Perils of Dating Celine

Cock-A-Voodoo-Doo

The Devil's Hairball

Like a Tramp Yelling at Trains (And Other Unpoetic
Noises)

The Crucifiction of Bastard Jesus
(Co-authored with Lindsay Crook)

Freak Fuck

Nympho Nurses' Ton-Up Terror (Mondo Perverso #1)

Zombie Cheerleaders on LSD (Mondo Perverso #2)

Star Whores: Return of the Dildo (Mondo Perverso #3)

Girl Gang Clusterfuck in Cell Block B (Mondo Perverso #4)

Cannibal She-Devils of the Umpopo Delta (Mondo Perverso #5)

Wino Women's Car Park Catfight (Mondo Perverso #6)

COMING IN 2024

Unfit for Human Consumption

Jack's Dead

Nonce!

Nun Meat Carnival

Go Bananas!

HEE HAW

PETER CAFFREY

1: THE GIRL IN THE BOX

As late afternoon turned to early evening and the day's light faded, so did the sobs of the girl in the box. Throughout the shack, a crimson tinge coloured the dusty air, the setting sun bleeding its last light through the smeared and stained windows. Hee Haw sat in his chair, eyes fixed on the wooden crate which hung suspended from a beam in the roof.

The day had started without any indication of its terrible climax. After rising early and enjoying a light breakfast, he'd gone out walking in the woodland. As noon approached and his thoughts turned to heading home for lunch, he heard children's voices drifting through the trees. They were laughing and shrieking as they played, care-free and unaware of his presence. Creeping closer, hidden by the foliage, he spied on them, as he usually did when he crossed paths with youngsters in the woods.

He liked to watch, fantasising about abusing their young, supple bodies. Concealed in the bushes, he'd daydream about grabbing one of them and taking them back to his shack. Pleasuring himself in his hiding place, he'd imagine raping and killing them as he jerked off.

1

Dressed in brilliant white, the boys and girls stood out from the woodland background as they chased each other, taunting and teasing in a friendly fashion. Hee Haw watched, licking his lips as he stroked his erect cock. Without warning, the relative quiet was overwhelmed by peeling church bells echoing through the trees from the village, the rolling noise added to by the children's elevated squeals of excitement.

They ran off towards the cacophony, cheering and whooping, punching the air in celebration. As their screams and shrieks faded in the distance, Hee Haw stood and zipped up his trousers, frustrated at the sudden end to his fantasy. Then he spotted her: a girl, young and innocent, dressed in a flowing white silk dress. Moving slowly through the trees, she glanced around but didn't appear to be frightened. If anything, she seemed at home with her solitude.

Before Hee Haw could take cover, she turned and looked straight at him, her face cracking into a smile as their eyes met.

'Hello,' she said, her tone friendly, as if greeting a friend.

'Hello there,' Hee Haw muttered, unsure how to react. 'What are you doing here all alone?'

'We were playing, my friends and I,' she replied. 'It's our first holy communion day, and they're having a lunch for us at the church, but everyone's gone, and I don't know where I am.'

'You don't know where the church is?' he asked.

'No. We—my family and I—only moved here a week ago, and I'm not sure where I am.'

Despite being lost and alone, she exuded a cheery confidence.

'Would you like me to show you the way?' he asked.

'Yes, please,' she said, placing her delicate hand in his when he proffered it.

Hee Haw led the girl off the path and through the boughs, heading deeper into the gloom of the wood, away from the church and her friends and relatives.

Now, many hours later, the evening's darkness enveloped his shack, an inky blackness creeping from the corners of the room. As it spread like a bruise, he allowed a smile to crawl across his lips.

Inside the box, the cramped conditions were pushing her body into a world of pain. Suffering immense agonies, both physical and emotional, she'd already lost control of her bodily functions. The intense stench hanging in the humid air served as evidence she'd soiled herself. A dark, tar-like syrup oozed from between the wooden slats and dripped to the floor, forming a viscous puddle of piss and liquid shit. Sniffing out the banquet, fat bluebottles buzzed around the spreading stain of faecal sludge.

It had been five or maybe six hours since he'd taken her. By now, her family and friends would be panicking. Those waiting at the church would have been irritated at first, rolling their eyes and tutting under their breath at her tardiness. The irritation would have changed to annoyance as they imagined her chatting to her friends, dallying in the woodland, while they awaited the start of the celebratory

3

luncheon. Eventually, the annoyance would have become anger as they mentally rehearsed a long lecture on the merits of punctuality. How long did it take for their anger to dissipate into an uncomfortable concern, then fear, a sickening terror overwhelming them as their darkest nightmare became a reality?

Thoughts of her suffering loved ones created a stirring in his groin, a flutter of excitement which made his balls tingle and his cock stiffen. He longed to be in the same room as her family, sharing their misery and torment, sobbing along with them in a fakery of mental anguish and despair. If he pretended to be a cripple, he could sit in a wheelchair, a blanket covering his groin, wanking while they wailed and wept and promised their favoured deities an unending list of sacrifices if she'd just walk through the door.

But she wouldn't walk through the door, not ever again, because she was with him, in the shack, in a box.

Chuckling to himself, Hee Haw shoved his hand into his pants, eager to masturbate. His bony fingers wrapped around his penis, avoiding contact with the festering boil on his shaft. He knew he needed to consult the doctor, but a crawling sense of shame prevented him from doing so. The infection made masturbation painful, but he struggled through the discomfort to achieve a moment of release.

Allowing thoughts of the girl's grieving parents to flood his mind, Hee Haw worked his cock harder, but as he approached his peak, a voice outside split the night air. It was shrill, authoritative, commanding in its timbre.

'Colin? Your dinner's ready!'

Hee Haw sighed, letting go of his throbbing cock despite the urge to shoot a string of spunk across the crate.

'Coming, Mother,' he shouted back, the irony not lost on him.

Leaning forward, his face so close to the box the ammonia-funk stench of her piss stung his eyes, he whispered, 'I'll be back, and when I am, we'll have games to play. Now, mind to keep quiet while I'm away, or I swear I'll bring such agonies down on you you'll welcome death with open arms.'

Standing, he rearranged his trousers so his hard-on wasn't obvious, and stepped outside. Locking the shack's door, he strolled towards the house.

In the kitchen the lamps were lit, their flames flickering, casting a sickly light into the murky evening darkness. Through the window, Hee Haw could see his father. The bald-headed prick sat at the table, his face decorated with a scowl. He'd be put out at having to wait for his supper. He might be the breadwinner, but Mother wouldn't let him start eating, not until the three of them were all seated.

His father was an embarrassment: sixty-six years old and stacking shelves in another man's store. He acted as if his job held some importance to society, but the worthless prick just put one can of beans on top of another can of beans, over and over again. He was a lackey, a minion, a performer of menial deeds.

As Colin entered the house, he heard his father growl, 'About time too. I've been working all day and I'm famished.'

'I just need to wash my hands,' Colin shouted, grinning as he imagined his father's grimace.

In the bathroom, dropping his trousers around his ankles, he pissed. Before flushing, he waddled over to the sink, his cock still hanging out, and turned on the tap. Wetting his fingers, he pulled back his foreskin and wiped away the sludgy film which coated his helmet. Before rinsing his fingers, he sniffed them. The grey slime had an odour of vinegar and wet dog. Next, he carefully wiped away the discharge weeping from the septic boil, before drying his prick on the hand towel. Then he tucked it away, zipped up, and flushed the toilet.

Leaning against the bathroom door, Colin slowly counted to one hundred, stifling a giggle as he thought of his father waiting to eat. The old bastard would be livid at the delay. Eventually, with a cocksure grin plastered on his face, he exited the bathroom and headed for the kitchen.

Dinner was not good, but then again, it never was. The cold, dry chicken and the over-cooked cabbage congealed on the plate like a septic sore. His father didn't seem to notice. He just shovelled the shit right into his big, fat, cunt of a mouth. Mother picked at hers, obvious irritation etched on her face.

Fork in hand, Colin pushed the food around his plate. His stomach turned slightly with disgust. It wasn't just the appearance of the food which stopped him eating; he was eager to get back to the girl. With a sigh, he put the cutlery down and pushed his chair back from the table.

'I'm not hungry, so I might as well leave,' he muttered. 'Anyway, I have more important things to do than sitting around here all night.'

'Can't you just be polite and wait until we've finished eating?' his mother snapped. 'What's so important you need to run away from us at the earliest opportunity?'

Colin shrugged.

'I bet it's wanking,' his father muttered. 'He's wanking out there.'

'So what if I am wanking?' Colin spat. 'What does it have to do with you? Maybe I like it in my shack because I don't have to suffer your boorish behaviour. If I hear one more story about the challenges of putting cans of beans onto a shelf, I swear to God I'll slash my wrists.'

'It's what brings money into this house,' his father declared with pomposity. 'Maybe I could reduce my working hours if you took responsibility for your own life. Isn't it about time you found a job and got a place of your own? You're nearly forty years old, Colin. How many men of your age still live with their parents?'

'I don't live *with* you,' Colin snapped.

'No,' his father said with a condescending grin. 'You live in an old outhouse in our garden; an outhouse which *we* own. You like to shout the odds about being independent, but you still come in here every day for your food, to get your clothes washed, to use the toilet and wipe your lazy arsehole. When I was your age, I was married and working extra jobs at night to pay for your sorry existence. But you? You just hang on to your mother's apron strings like a bloody retard.'

'Hush now,' Mother said, more in hope than expectation the exchange would end.

'Fuck you,' Colin snarled at his father. 'If I'm such an inconvenience, I'll move out tomorrow, and when I'm gone, you can reduce the hours you work, but you won't be able to reduce how pathetic you are.'

'But you won't move out, will you, Colin?' his father said smugly. 'You won't do *anything* because you never do. You're all talk, boy.'

'Just you wait and see,' Colin snapped. 'It won't be long now, and everyone will know my name. The whole world will know about Hee Haw.'

'That's my point,' his father bellowed. 'You're old enough to be a parent yourself, and yet you still refer to yourself using a childish name and pretend to be someone you're not. You're a fucking fantasist, son.'

'I'm not Colin, not anymore,' Colin screamed. 'You killed Colin, you bastard. The little boy is dead. Only Hee Haw remains.'

'Get a fucking job, move out, and you can call yourself whatever you want, *Colin*, but until then you'll show me respect in my own house,' his father said sternly, waving his finger in admonishment.

'Please, that's enough,' Mother muttered, standing and collecting up the dinner plates.

'I will do something, you'll see,' Colin snarled. 'I'll do something big, and then ... you'll eat your fucking words.'

With that, he stormed out through the back door and into the night.

2: ALL TIED UP

Hee Haw slammed the shack door, locking it behind him. Dragging his chair next to the box, he sat, staring at the wooden crate, but his thoughts weren't on the girl.

Rage bubbled inside his guts as the confrontation with his father replayed in his head. How dare the old bastard talk down to him. He had no clue about his capabilities, no understanding of his ambitions and plans, nor of the dark vein of human emotion which drove him. The interferences of malevolent beings and their diabolic plans didn't even come into the old man's thinking. Through his father's ignorant and blinkered eyes, everything was linear and logical, black and white. Nothing existed in between.

The older generation, his fucking father's generation, thought people only existed to live mediocre lives with menial jobs, wasting their time until they died a nobody and were buried alongside their humdrum friends and families in the local cemetery. Banality was all his father knew. In truth, it was all he deserved. The silly old cunt had saved a space in his tedious world for Colin, but Colin was no more. The child of monotony was dead; now only Hee Haw remained.

For Hee Haw, things were different. The world was a psychedelic cosmos, a vibrant place in a constant state of flux. In such a space, he was free to expand, and his destiny was one of notoriety, of infamy. His name would be mentioned in hushed tones by those who understood the true depths of his dreadful capabilities. Away from the moral and emotional confines of the *status quo*, Hee Haw would be revered, forever feared.

Sitting, brooding, Hee Haw's thoughts were interrupted by a muffled whimper coming from the box.

'Hello?'

The girl's voice was frail, cracking with emotion. By now, she'd be crumbling under the strain, struggling to survive the hellish nightmare thrust upon her. Hee Haw held his breath, buying himself a few seconds to consider the best response.

'Hello? Is anyone there?' she whimpered, the desperation in her voice spreading a smile across Hee Haw's face.

Standing, he untied the rope and slowly lowered the wooden crate to the floor before snatching the lid open.

The girl blinked against the ingress of light, her eyes wide and black and startled, oozing a depth of inner terror. He'd seen the same look of dread before, many years ago, when a scaffolding truck reversed over next door's tortoiseshell. With its guts squashed out of its arsehole, the cat died a slow and agonising death in the gutter, its terrified eyes fixed on him as he'd squatted next to it, watching its life ebb away.

'What do you want?' he snarled.

Blinking, a pained grimace on her face, the girl muttered, 'I was wondering what you were going to do to me?'

'What am I going to do to you?' Hee Haw snarled. 'Unspeakable things, fucking terrible things. Imagine the darkest, nastiest, most humiliating abuse a human could be forced to suffer. Well, what I'll do to you will be ten times worse.'

The girl nodded, her eyes fixed on his. Despite the threat, she didn't display any visible signs of fear. If anything, she appeared to be trapped in a moment of hesitancy as she gazed up at him, as if wanting to ask something else.

'What?' Hee Haw snapped, impatience gnawing at his mood as he loomed above her like a cat over an injured bird.

'Why?' she asked.

He frowned, confused by her reply.

'Why what?'

'Why are you going to do unspeakable things to me? What have I ever done to you?'

A surge of discomfort pulsed through Hee Haw's body. It wasn't the question which triggered something inside him. It was the girl's attitude. The way she asked the question was as if they were debating some philosophical conundrum rather than her pleading for mercy. He wanted her to snivel and beg, not discuss the fucking situation.

'I'm doing them because I can,' he said abruptly, 'and I'll tell you something else: if you question me, things will only get worse for you.'

'I'm sorry,' she whispered. 'Honestly, I'm not questioning you, *Colin*.'

As she said his name, he shuddered.

'Why did you call me that?'

The girl shrugged.

'I thought it was your name. I heard it when you were called in for dinner.'

'I'm not Colin,' he spat, pushing his face closer to hers, his breathing so aggressive it wafted away the strands of hair falling over her face. 'Colin is dead. He is no more. I am Hee Haw.'

The girl's face morphed into a smile, and she giggled.

'What's so fucking funny?' he snarled.

'Hee Haw,' she said. 'Why do you call yourself that? Do you like donkeys, Colin?'

'Don't call me Colin, you dirty cunt. I'm not Colin.'

She fell silent for a moment, bowing her head, shamed by the admonishment. When she looked back up, the childish grin had vanished.

'But do you like donkeys?' she asked again with sincerity.

'Why the fuck do you think I like donkeys?'

'Because Hee Haw is the noise a donkey makes, isn't it?'

'No,' Hee Haw said sternly. 'It's the noise of death and destruction, of war against the overwhelming tide of mundanity. It's the battle cry of the infamous and the extraordinary when they rally against the onslaught of inanity. It's the echoing screams of the unborn and the disenfranchised souls which resonate in the fires of hell when those who have been downtrodden and dismissed overthrow the dullards and the nobodies. It is the death-knell of the mediocre.'

The girl nodded.

'But really, it's a donkey noise, isn't it?' she said in a matter-of-fact manner.

Raising his hand, Hee Haw feigned to strike, but the girl didn't flinch.

'I'm sorry if I upset you,' she said with innocence. 'I'm only telling you what I think. It sounds like the noise a donkey makes.'

'Well, I don't give a shit what you think,' he replied. 'Shut the fuck up about donkeys or I'll hurt you so bad you'll wish you were dead.'

'Sorry,' she muttered, her eyes downcast. 'I didn't mean to make you angry. And please, don't hurt me. I don't want to be hurt. I'm trying to behave properly, and don't like to question my elders, but there's one last thing I'd like to say.'

The girl paused, awaiting permission to continue.

'What?' Hee Haw snapped.

'I was thinking, it would be best if you tied me up.'

Staring at the girl in disbelief, Hee Haw asked, 'You want me to tie you up?'

'I might escape,' she replied nonchalantly. 'You probably should tie me up. Think about it: if I get away and tell people you snatched me, they'll come after you.'

'You won't escape,' Hee Haw sneered. 'If you try, I'll kill you.'

The girl nodded.

'It would be for the best.'

'You ... you want to die?' he asked with incredulity.

'Oh, no, I don't want to die.' The girl's tone wasn't pleading or fearful. If anything, she seemed detached. 'I meant it would be best for you to kill me if I tried to escape. If you didn't and I managed to get away, I'd raise the alarm and people would hunt you down.'

Again, the girl's attitude triggered an uneasy sensation and his anxiety increased.

'Shut up,' he hissed.

'Sorry. It's just that I wanted—'

'I said shut the fuck up. If you keep talking, I won't ever let you go.'

'But you can't let me go, ever,' she said without emotion.

'What makes you think that?' Hee Haw asked, surprised at her reaction.

'The same reason you'll need to kill me if I try to escape. If you let me go, I'll tell everyone what you did, and they'll come looking for you. Imagine them swarming around you, brandishing weapons, the dogs barking and snarling and straining at the leash, eager to get at you and tear your flesh apart. The mob would beat you half to death. They'd inflict horrors on you like you can't imagine. You wouldn't survive. That's why you can't let me go.'

Her words weren't a threat or a warning. They were simple facts. Hee Haw's stomach knotted as panic flooded his guts.

'You don't know who I am, or where you are,' he snarled, despite an overwhelming sense of

15

vulnerability invading his thoughts. 'Even if you managed to get away, you'd never find me again.'

'It wouldn't be too hard,' the girl said. 'We're close to the church where I made my first communion. We only walked for ten or fifteen minutes, and our pace was quite slow, so we're not too far away. I know your name is Colin, and you live with your mother.'

'She's not my mother,' Hee Haw hissed. 'She's my ... servant.'

'Oh, I'm sorry. It's just you called her Mother, but maybe it's her nickname. Either way, someone will know who you are. All things considered, it would probably be best if you tied me up.'

Deep in his guts, an unpleasant churning sensation generated pulses of nausea. Fighting the urge to spew, he felt a tremor of fear grating deep inside his belly. She was the victim, not him, so why was he the one suffering?

'I *could* let you go if you kept your mouth shut,' he said, struggling to regain his composure. 'If you told anyone about me, I'd find you and deliver the slowest, most agonising death I could. Then I'd kill your family too, every single one of them.'

The girl shook her head.

'It's not an option,' she said with a strange calmness. 'By now, people will have missed me. They'll want to know where I've been. They won't accept me keeping silent. Sorry, but I don't think you have any other choice. You should tie me up.'

'You don't get to tell me what to do,' he said with contempt. 'I'm Hee Haw.'

Slamming the lid of the crate, he paced the floor of the shack, limbs tingling with an electric energy driven by fear, or rage, or some other emotion he couldn't fathom.

This wasn't how things should be. He was in charge, not her. He called the shots. She should be a quivering wreck, a frightened child begging for her life. Instead, she had the audacity to tell him how to do things.

A burning sensation of shame flushed across his skin. He wouldn't let a child tell him what to do. He'd teach her to stick her nose where it didn't belong. If she wanted tying up, he'd tie her up alright. He'd tie her up so tight, she'd wish she hadn't opened her stupid fucking mouth.

Searching the shack, he found a length of rope. Hacking it in two, he stomped across to the box and flung the lid open.

'Give me your fucking hands,' he demanded.

Without a word, the girl held out her arms. Wrapping the rope around her wrists, he jerked the ends hard to make the process as uncomfortable as possible. Despite his efforts to hurt her, the girl didn't react, her eyes following every movement his fingers made as he tied the knot.

'Feet,' he snapped.

With her hands bound, she struggled to move inside the box. Hee Haw knew he should have tied her feet first, but he wasn't about to admit his error. He knew he'd got it wrong, and he knew she knew he'd got it wrong too.

Standing in silence, he waited until she'd struggled into a position which allowed access to her ankles, before roughly tying them.

As he swung the lid of the crate closed, she called out.

'Wait! Haven't you forgotten something?'

Pausing to swallow back his rage, he flipped the lid open again.

'What now?'

'You might want to tie me around the neck. If you looped a rope through one of the slats in the crate, it would be extremely uncomfortable. I wouldn't be able to sit or lie down properly. I wouldn't be able to sleep. It would be an on-going torture.'

'You're suggesting I tie you around the neck?' Hee Haw asked with surprise.

'Yes,' she muttered. 'Like a dog.'

'Don't think you can become my friend by trying to be helpful,' he snapped. 'I'm not a friendly sort of man.'

The girl's eyes dropped to stare at the bottom of the crate.

'Oh, no sir,' she said, as if in repentance. 'I would never dream of doing that.'

'I'm going to rape and kill you,' Hee Haw hissed. 'I have a whole load of terrors I'm going to unleash on you.'

'I dare say you have, sir,' she said, her voice almost a whimper. 'I'm sorry.'

Hee Haw set about searching the shack, but he couldn't find any more rope. Spotting a length of electrical flex, he grabbed the wire. It would have to do.

Looping it through the side of the crate, he wrapped the ends around the girl's throat and pulled them tight. The skin on her neck pinched as the cable cut in.

'Can you breathe?' Hee Haw asked.

The girl nodded.

'I don't want you dying,' he said with a twisted smile, 'at least, not until I've done what I want to do with you.'

Slamming the lid of the box, he took hold of the rope and once more hoisted the crate off the floor.

3: ALONE IN THE WOODS

As the first fingers of grey light crept through the dusty windows, Hee Haw struggled from his bed. Outside, the world was silent aside from the early morning chatter of bird song. Dragging on his clothes, he crossed the room and stood by the suspended crate, his ear close to a gap in the slats. He could hear her breathing, her inhalations and exhalations slow and shallow. She'd survived the night.

Pulling on his boots and tucking his hunting knife into the back of his belt, he unlocked the door and stepped outside. Despite the brightness, the air carried a chill, the sun not being high enough to spread its warmth. Hee Haw moved slowly towards the woodland, placing his feet down gently to minimise any noise.

Edging into the trees, the bird song died away and silence enveloped him. The golden flickering caused by the rising sun glinting through the branches dappled the dew-soaked foliage. Aside from the dancing sparks of light, he could see no movement. Everything was still. If a search party was out looking for the girl, they weren't in the right place.

Hee Haw made his way through the woodland, moving stealthily until he reached its far edge.

Beyond the tree-line lay open fields, and in the distance, the local village slumbered. There were no signs of unusual activity: no men with bloodhounds, no angry mobs, no agitated locals, no signs of the frenzied activity he'd expect if the authorities were trying to locate a missing child.

Wherever the powers-that-be had focussed their search, it was a long way from his shack.

Despite being marginally reassured by the lack of commotion, he still moved with care, minimising any noise he might make as he headed back through the woods towards home.

On Mondays, his father covered the late shift at work. Usually, Hee Haw wouldn't go into the house until after the old bastard had left for town, but today was different. He wanted to check the morning newspaper to find out what the police were doing to locate the missing girl. Did they suspect foul play, or were they still checking with friends and family to see if anyone knew where she might be?

While an understanding of police activity would be useful, Hee Haw was intrigued to see how he was being portrayed by the mass-media. Were they whipping the populace into a state of terror by claiming a monster was on the loose, or was their goal to minimise panic by painting him as an opportunistic kidnapper?

Opening the back door, he walked into the kitchen. Seeing him, his mother smiled.

'Tea, Colin?'

Colin nodded as he sat at the table. His father sighed in a dramatic fashion but didn't acknowledge his son's presence, his focus remaining on the newspaper.

As his mother poured his drink, Colin asked, 'Is that today's paper?'

'It is,' his father said, his tone joyless.

'Can I have a quick look?'

Once more, his father sighed.

'As you can see, I'm reading it.'

Colin fought back the urge to tell his father to fuck himself, instead adopting a more conciliatory tone.

'Sorry,' he muttered. 'It's just I wanted to have a quick look at the Jobs section...'

His father lowered the paper and grinned.

'Do you hear this, Mother?' he asked with a sarcastic sneer. 'Colin suddenly wants to find a job. Have a look out of the window and tell me if you see any pigs flying past.'

'Don't start this early in the day,' Mother chided.

Folding the paper, his father threw it onto the table.

'Take it,' he said as he rose from his chair. 'I need to get ready for work.'

Father headed upstairs and Mother cleared the table of the breakfast things. As she washed the dishes, Colin checked the newspaper. The main front-page story reported on a political summit being held to address environmental sustainability. A side-bar teased an exposé of a prominent celebrity's gambling addiction. There wasn't a single mention of the missing girl.

Frustrated, Colin flicked through the pages, the dullness of the various stories making it obvious yesterday had been a slow news day. Despite the lack of spicy reportage, the kidnapping hadn't been given any column inches. Was the newspaper an early edition, printed before the abduction came to light? Maybe the police were refraining from announcing a manhunt until the family exhausted every potential outcome, checking with friends and neighbours to see whether she'd turned up. Often, on television shows, the police insisted on waiting twenty-four hours before taking action when a person went missing, but would they wait that long if it was a child?

'Shall I make you some breakfast?' Mother asked as she ran a cloth across the work surfaces.

'No,' Colin muttered, standing. 'I've got stuff to do, errands to run.'

'Like what?' she asked, but he was already out of the door.

Returning to the shack, Hee Haw lowered the crate and opened the lid. The girl lay in a contorted position, blinking, the grime on her face streaked where tears had run down her cheeks. A raw, painful weal stood out on her neck where the flex had rubbed against her skin.

Loosening the wire, he allowed her to shift into a more comfortable position.

'Do you want anything?' he asked.

She shook her head.

'Are you sure? You won't last long without water or food. I don't think you need any food, not yet. You'll only shit in the box if you eat too much.'

'You're right,' she croaked, struggling to speak. 'The lack of nutrition will ensure I grow weaker, becoming more pliable to your will.'

Hee Haw shuddered. There was something strange about her, something he couldn't put his finger on which he found unsettling. She didn't have the strength nor the wit to fight back, yet she was bereft of fear, almost oblivious to the peril in which she found herself.

'Do you want some water?'

Again, she shook her head.

'You need to drink water,' he insisted. 'I don't want you dying on me, not before I've had my fun.'

'Okay,' she muttered. 'Please could I have some water?'

At the sink, he filled a chipped, stained cup and took it across to the box. Still partially tied, she opened her mouth and gulped down the liquid as he poured it from the cup.

'More?' he asked, and she nodded.

Unzipping his trousers, he pulled out his cock and urinated, the piss overflowing the rim of the cup and cascading to the floor.

As he moved the cup towards her, she closed her mouth, her lips clamped tight.

'Drink it,' he snapped with aggression, his instruction an obvious command.

Her eyes glazed as a sheen of tears built up, her lips pressed shut so hard her face twitched.

'Fucking drink it, you cunt,' he snarled, thrusting the cup of piss towards her.

She opened her mouth, tears sparkling as they oozed between her closed eyelids, and he poured the warm, salty urine into her mouth.

Gagging and heaving, she gurgled as bubbles of piss blew out of her nostrils. Struggling to swallow, rivulets of yellow waste dribbled from her chin.

'Don't spill it,' he growled. 'You need it to stay alive, so get it down you.'

With her face contorted in a grimace of revulsion, she swallowed.

Hee Haw laughed and tossed the cup into the sink. After rummaging in a cupboard, he moved to his chair, a whetstone in his hand. Pulling out his hunting knife, he began to sharpen the blade.

'Why did you snatch me?' the girl asked, her voice frail. 'Is it because you don't have any friends?'

'I have friends. I have plenty of friends. They live inside my head.'

Hee Haw grinned as he honed the blade, pleased with his response. He hadn't planned to say it; the words just came out.

'I think that sounds like an excuse for being alone,' the girl said.

Hee Haw stopped circling the knife's blade on the stone.

'I don't give a fuck what you think,' he spat. 'You're nothing. You're a little child, a fucking infant. Your opinion means nothing to me. I am a man possessed, driven by an internal diabolical fire, a burning hatred for this planet and all the maggots who reside on it. When you hear the sound of Hee

Haw, your days are numbered. You *will* hear my terrible roar.'

Pausing for a moment, he glared at her with contempt.

'Anyway, don't worry your pretty little head about me. Tell me all about you. For starters, what's your name?'

'What do you want me to be called?' she asked, the fake innocence with which she spoke verging on mockery.

Hee Haw once more felt the prickle of anxiety creeping across his skin. Her attitude didn't match with that of a victim. Her reply teetered on being flirtatious, as if she thought it was all a game.

'This isn't a fucking game,' he said, pointing the knife at her for emphasis. 'You're in real danger.'

'I dare say I am,' she whispered.

'You *are* in danger, so be a good girl and tell me your fucking name.'

'Do you like the name Mary ... as in the Virgin Mary?'

Hee Haw sighed.

'Is your name Mary?'

'Do *you* like the name Mary?'

'Not really,' he replied.

'My name's not Mary,' she said with an apologetic tone. 'What do you think of Gloria?'

'Just answer the fucking question,' he growled, glaring at her, his eyes burning with rage. 'Believe me, I'm going to hurt you if you mess me around.'

'I want to tell you—'

'I'll find out your fucking name,' he interjected. 'Trust me; I only need to watch the news this evening and they'll be reporting on your disappearance. I'll also find out where your family lives, and after I've fucked you and dumped your body, I'll go fuck and kill them too.'

There was a moment of silence before she spoke again.

'Do you like the name Alice?'

'It's okay.'

'I'm Alice.'

Hee Haw looked up, his face twisted into a grimace.

Well, Alice, if that is your name, this is how things are going to be. Next time I ask a fucking question, you answer it. Understand?'

'I understand,' she whimpered.

'I'm not fucking around. I'll hurt you if you start any nonsense.'

'I understand.' Her voice grew weaker, more timid.

Hee Haw returned his attention to the knife, slowly circling the blade on the whetstone before testing the edge with his thumb.

'So, when I found you, what were you doing all alone in the woods?' he asked.

'I was playing ... with my friends,' she whispered. 'We'd finished our first communion and went to play, before the luncheon. It was time to go back, but I stopped to tie my shoelace, and when I looked up, they'd gone. I think they went back to the church, to their families, but before I could catch up with them, you grabbed me.'

Hee Haw tilted his head, his eyes fixed on hers. Feeling awkward, she looked away.

'And your family?' he asked.

'What about them?'

'Do you think they've missed you?'

'Definitely,' she replied. 'I'd imagine they're out right now, searching for me, doing everything they can to find me.'

Hee Haw laughed.

'Yes, Alice; I'd imagine the same thing too. I think we'd all imagine our families would be out searching if we went missing. I mean, think about it: what possible reason would they have not to be out looking for you?'

'They'll be looking for me,' she said with confidence. 'They'll be out looking, and they won't stop until they find me. Even if it takes forever, they'll never stop looking.'

'You think so?'

Alice nodded.

'I know so.'

'Well, little Alice, here's my advice: hang on to that thought. Hang on to it for as long as you can.'

With that, he stood, slammed the lid shut and hoisted the crate off the floor.

4: OVERWHELMING SILENCE

Colin sat at the kitchen table, twiddling his thumbs. As his mother fussed around the cooker, preparing the evening meal, he tried to present an air of nonchalance, but the rising tension tearing at the fabric of his being made it difficult.

Usually, when his father worked the late shift, Colin ate early, ensuring he was gone before the old bastard returned. It was the one evening he could escape the boring conversations and inevitable snipes and squabbles. However, tonight was different: he wanted something. His father had been in town, at the store, and if there'd been any gossip about the missing girl, he would have heard it.

'Shall I serve your supper now, Colin?' his mother asked, expecting him to perform his usual eat-and-run routine.

'No,' he mumbled. 'I might as well wait for the old man to get back. He should be here any minute.'

While surprised, she said nothing.

Colin glanced at the clock. His father was usually home by now, unless something was happening in town. Had the store staff been asked to join a search party? The old man was a nosy bastard and would leap at any chance to interfere in someone else's misfortune. Maybe he was out, right now, sweeping through the streets and lanes, searching for Alice.

It had to happen. The inaction had dragged on for too long. At some point, someone would start looking, surely?

Earlier in the afternoon, he'd once more crept through the trees, arriving at the edge of the woodland. The village still appeared to be quiet: there were no signs of unusual activity, nor any evidence the police were there. No one was searching the woods, and if any dog teams or helicopters had been deployed, he saw neither hide nor hair of them. Things were normal, as if a child hadn't gone missing. But were they too normal?

Gazing out of the window into the encroaching darkness, he saw the lamp of his father's bicycle weaving up the driveway. The old fucker was home. The urge to go out and meet him, to quiz him about his day, ate away at Colin, but it was critical his interest in the missing girl wasn't too obvious. Sitting and waiting, time dragged.

Walking into the kitchen, his father pecked Mother on the cheek before settling at the table. Glancing at Colin, he raised his eyebrows and smirked but didn't speak.

'Did you have a good day, Dad?' Colin asked, his face feeling unnatural as he forced a fake smile.

'What are you after?' his father replied without warmth.

'Nothing,' Colin said, shrugging. 'I just wondered if you had a good day.'

It sounded false, and inside he cringed, but his impatience was rampant. Waiting for his father to volunteer the information wasn't an option.

'Are you after money?' his father asked with suspicion.

Turning to face his wife, he added, 'He's after money, isn't he?'

'I'm not after money,' Colin muttered.

'If you want money, you should get a job like the rest of us.'

'I've been looking for work, but no one's hiring,' Colin said, fighting the urge to tell his father to fuck himself, before storming out. But he couldn't. He needed to know if anyone had mentioned the missing girl.

'I can ask if they have any vacancies at the store,' his father said dismissively, 'but you'll need to turn up on time and watch your attitude. I have to work there after you've gone.'

'I don't want to work at ... never mind,' Colin said. 'Anything exciting happen today?'

'The corned beef is on sale,' his father replied. 'I can't understand why people want imported, canned meat, but they do. I must have restocked the shelf six or seven times. You can make any old crap half price and folks will buy it.'

Mother served dinner. Colin looked down at the plate. He had no idea what it was supposed to be. An oily brown slick spread across the patterned porcelain, and pieces of something sinuous rose from the unappetising gloop. On one side of the dirty puddle sat a pile of grey mashed potatoes. How the fuck did she get them to turn grey?

'So, there's nothing happening in town?' Colin asked, prodding at one of the gristly lumps with his fork.

Slurping up the sludge, his father shook his head.

'Nothing ever happens around here,' he gurgled through a mouthful of mash and greasy gravy. 'I think one of the regulars said something about her cat going missing, but after a few nights it came home. Listen, Colin, I've been working all day and I'm tired. I want to eat my dinner in peace, so let's cut the small-talk. If you need money, you're going to have to find yourself a job. As I said before, I can ask at the store, but you'd better not let me down.'

'I don't want your money,' Colin whined. 'I was just being polite, taking an interest in your day, but if you're going to act like a twat, I'm off.'

Pushing his plate away, he rose and marched towards the back door.

'Don't call me a twat, not in my own house,' his father roared. Mother added something, but the sound of the door slamming drowned out her inane mumbling.

Hee Haw strode through the darkness and entered the shack. Locking the door behind himself, he lowered the crate to the floor and lifted the lid. Alice blinked as if momentarily blinded.

'Don't even think about lying to me,' he barked. 'Tell me about your family. Who was waiting for you at the church?'

'What do you ... what do you want to know?' she stuttered, shocked at the sudden and aggressive questioning.

'Answer my fucking question,' Hee Haw snarled. 'Who was waiting for you?'

For a moment, Alice's facial expression faltered from her normal placidity, a furrow of concern spreading across her brow.

'My father ... and my mother. Oh, my aunt as well, and my cousins.'

'What's your aunt's name?' he snapped.

'Why do want to know?' she asked, her question almost a whimper.

Hee Haw raised his arm and balled his hand, ready to punch, the threat intended to solicit an answer.

'Clara,' Alice spluttered, her eyes fixed on his clenched fist.

'And your cousins?'

'Edmond and ... Emily.'

'So, when your parents, Edmond, Emily and Aunt Clarissa realised you weren't coming back, what do you think they did?'

'Aunt Clara,' Alice whispered.

'*What?*'

'Aunt Clara; you said Aunt Clarissa.'

Hee Haw sighed. She'd spotted he'd used the wrong name. He'd tested her too soon, rather than leaving it for a while so she'd forget what she'd told him. Smothering his anger at his own impatience, he sneered, 'Clara, Clarissa, it's all the fucking same. What did they think when you didn't return?'

'I don't know,' she said, the faux innocence once more on display. 'I guess they must have been worried, maybe searched for a while, and then informed the authorities.'

'You think so?'

Hee Haw's question was aggressive, a verbal challenge as she cowered in the crate.

'Yes, they would have told people I was missing. I'm sure they would. Why do you ask?'

Hee Haw turned and walked to the other side of the shack. It just didn't add up. He'd taken Alice on Sunday lunchtime. Now it was Monday evening, but there didn't appear to be anyone searching for her, no one in town was talking about a missing child, and the newspapers weren't reporting her disappearance. Something was wrong. Surely, in a case of child abduction, time was of the essence.

There was one possible explanation; the only explanation Hee Haw could think of. Alice was a runaway. She wasn't with the other children. She'd been on her own. No one missed her, because she hadn't disappeared from the church. Wherever she'd gone missing from, it wasn't around here, and it wasn't in the last few days. She might have vanished months ago, and her family and friends were looking for her on the other side of the country. If it was the case, it went some way towards explaining her strange attitude. She'd hardened up during her weeks or even months on the run.

However, there was still one thing which didn't make sense: her dress. She wore a flowing white, silk gown, the sort girls wore when making their first communion. If she'd been living rough, it wouldn't be clean and pristine. She'd struggle to survive the cold nights in such attire. It was the time of year many parishes celebrated the ritual, so she could have stolen it from a washing line.

If she was a runaway, no one would come looking for her. She was, to all intents and purposes, his to do with as he wished.

Walking back over to the crate, he peered in. Her usual confidence had deserted her as she trembled, trying her best to recede into the corner of the box. An evil grin cracked his face, a snigger escaping his contorted mouth.

'No one is looking for you, are they?'

'They *are* looking for me,' Alice said quietly, but her tone indicated a level of uncertainty.

'No one is looking for you,' Hee Haw crowed. 'There's no one searching the woods, the village is dead, and the only thing they're talking about in town is a missing fucking cat. Trust me, Alice, no one cares about you, not your mother, not your father, not Aunt Clarissa and certainly not Edmund nor Emily, if they even exist.'

'It's Aunt Clara,' Alice said, an edge of defiance creeping into her voice. 'And they *are* looking for me.'

'Then why is there no activity out there? Is it because you're a dirty little liar?'

'I'm not a liar,' Alice sobbed, the tinge of bravado she seemed to be building suddenly crumbling.

'Well, if you're not, why is no one searching?'

For a moment, Alice closed her eyes, her face twitching as if she were about to dissolve into tears, but she slowly opened them again, her composure returned.

'Before we moved here, when we lived in the city, a girl at my school went missing,' she said. 'The police didn't make any appeals, there was no press coverage, nothing. We were instructed to keep quiet and tell no one she had been snatched. They said kidnappers thrive off notoriety, and if they're ignored, they react and make mistakes. Sure enough, after a few days of no coverage or activity, the police caught the man and freed the girl. The silence spooked him, and as a result he made a foolish move. Trust me: they're out there and they're playing with you. They're coming with dogs and guns. They're coming for you.'

'Bullshit,' Hee Haw spat. 'You were in the woods, alone. You don't have any friends, not around here. You don't have any family. No one has reported you missing, and now, you're mine.'

Alice's eyes sparkled with tears.

'They're looking for me,' she cried, showing despair for the first time since being grabbed.

Hee Haw laughed, his cackle growing in intensity as his mirth exploded.

'No one cares about you, little Alice,' he jeered.

'They'll get you,' she shouted. 'They're coming, and they will get you.'

'Shut your mouth,' Hee Haw snarled. 'Shut your fucking mouth or I'll hurt you.'

Falling silent, she bowed her head, avoiding eye contact.

'I'm sorry,' she whispered.

36

'I said shut up, or I'll chop your ears off.'

With her head still down, her body shivering, she sobbed, before mumbling, 'Instead of cutting off my ears, you could...'

Hee Haw glared at her. Trembling in the crate, she was the victim, but it didn't feel that way. There was an element of mockery in her attitude, as if she refused to take his threats seriously. She questioned everything he did.

'I could what?' he barked.

Alice sighed, as if she were the adult and he was a little child pestering her with pointless questions.

'Instead of chopping off my ears, maybe you should slice off my eyelids.'

Hee Haw paused, astounded at her response. '*What?*'

'Rather than chopping off my ears, you could slice off my eyelids,' she repeated.

'Why the fuck would I do that?'

Hee Haw's face twisted into a grimace of disgust as he thought about what she'd said.

'If you sliced off my eyelids, I wouldn't be able to sleep,' Alice explained, her tone slightly condescending. 'It would be another torment to make what's left of my short life truly miserable. As well as the overall inconvenience of not being able to close my eyes, the physical impediment would be significant. It wouldn't take long for my corneal epithelia to dry and crack, and the cells would slough off. Once that happened, the stroma would ulcerate, my eyeballs becoming septic and effectively rotting in their sockets. Not only would I lose my sight, but a degree of necrosis would soon become established. Slicing off my eyelids would not only be more agonising and debilitating than cutting off my ears, but it would also prove you're a true monster.'

Hee Haw stared at Alice, his mouth hanging open.

'How old are you?' he asked.

'Nine,' she replied.

'Nine? How the fuck do you know stuff like that at nine?'

'Stuff like what?' Alice asked.

'Stuff like the corneal whatsitcalled.'

'I read ... a lot,' Alice said. 'I don't have any friends, so I spend my time with books.'

'All the learning in the world won't do you any good,' he said dismissively.

'Obviously,' she replied. Again, her intonation seemed designed to humiliate him.

Leaning over the edge of the box to glare into Alice's eyes, he asked, 'If you have no friends, who were you playing with in the woods?'

Alice looked up, her face a picture of innocence.

'They were children from the church. I know them, but they're not friends, not real friends. If they were real friends, they wouldn't have left me alone in the woods. They wouldn't have run off and abandoned me, prizing chocolate cake and fizzy pop above my safety. They wouldn't have left me to be snatched by you.'

Hee Haw reached across the box and, grabbing the electrical flex, jerked it tighter around Alice's neck.

'There's a difference between learning stuff and being smart,' he whispered. 'If you'd kept your mouth shut, I would have hacked off one of your ears, but now I'm going to cut off both your fucking eyelids.'

'It's for the best,' she croaked. 'You know it makes sense.'

5: THE DOGS DO BARK

Hee Haw tossed and turned in his bed, desperate for sleep to smother him with its comforting embrace. The cold, waxy sheets clung to his body, adhered with a film of sweat. Tired and befuddled, something nagged at the back of his mind, denying him the peace he craved. Through the haze of somnolence, he'd heard something unusual in the shack, an unwelcome sound which haunted his thoughts. Was it some lingering fragment of a disturbed dream, or had it come to him in a waking moment?

Outside, a storm was building, the wind howling as the drumming of rain skittered on the roof, but inside the shack, things were quiet. Were they too quiet? Laying in the dark, he listened intently but couldn't detect whatever had woken him.

He was at home, in his own bed, yet he sensed something malevolent in the air. The atmosphere felt off-kilter and otherworldly. Unable to identify the source of his discomfort, he was at least thankful he could no longer hear the sound.

Breathing deep and slow, concentrating on his inhalations and exhalations, he waited for the mists of sleep to wash over him. Drifting towards the spiralling haze of dreamtime, his mind filling with blurred memories and shards of fantasies unfulfilled, he heard the sound again.

A laugh, twisted and malicious, crept through the shack; a tinkling sound of mockery oozing from the box. It sent a chill crawling across his skin, gnawing down into his flesh, sinking so deep it touched his bones with an unpleasant frostiness.

Petrified in the moment, time dragged as the laughter swirled inside his head. It seemed to last an age, a tortuously unending moment of uneasiness, before fading. As the shack fell silent again, Hee Haw couldn't relax. If anything, the quiet was worse than the laughter.

Tension built in the pit of his guts as he waited, trembling, listening for the inevitable return of the sound. He knew it would start again, despite him wishing for nothing but tranquillity. He knew she'd not let him rest.

Fucking Alice: she was the victim, *his* victim, so how was she getting into his head? Her plight was perilous, and he expected her behaviour to reflect the terror she'd be experiencing. He'd understand if she were weeping, begging for mercy, pleading for her life, but instead the bitch was sniggering. She had nothing to laugh about.

Outside, the wind howled like a chorus of banshees wailing their morbid lamentations. Dragging himself up in bed, Hee Haw listened more intently, his focus on the noises seeping in from outside the shack. If the storm could sound like haunting voices, then surely it wasn't beyond reason it might recreate a spiteful giggle?

'Pull yourself together,' he muttered, keeping his voice quiet to ensure Alice wouldn't hear, but even as he tried to calm his jangling nerves, the laughter started again, coming from the box in short, explosive bursts, as if she struggled to suppress her mirth.

'Shut up,' Hee Haw shouted, unable to control the flutter of anxiety in his voice. 'Shut up, right now, or ... or you know what I'll do to you.'

As he uttered the threat, a wave of doubt washed over him. Did she know what he'd do to her? Did she even care? Instead of begging and pleading for her pitiful life, she was goading him. If she were afraid, truly afraid, mockery would be the last thing on her mind.

Maybe she did know what he'd do to her. Maybe she knew he'd do nothing. Despite the threat, he wasn't certain he'd be able to see things through. He'd snatched her to live out his fantasy, to rape and murder, but he hadn't touched her. Not yet. Why did he feel so uncertain, so ... afraid?

The shack once more fell silent, the laughter stopping, and from outside the noise of the storm increased.

Laying down and turning onto his side, he willed himself to sleep, but again he heard a laugh, albeit a brief one. Then she spoke, her voice a pervading hiss which sent an unpleasant tingling sensation up the back of his neck, as if an army of spiders crawled across his body.

'Can you hear them, Hee Haw?' she giggled. 'Listen carefully, listen well. Can you hear them?

The hounds are baying. They have your scent and they're closing in, following your trail, surrounding you. They're coming for you, like I said they would. They're coming to get you.'

Hee Haw sat up again, straining to listen. His heart beat with such a ferocity, he could feel the pulse in his temples. Outside, the wind whistled through the trees and the splattering of rain intensified, but he couldn't hear any dogs. She giggled again, her mockery assured and confident. Maybe she'd heard something: dogs barking in the distance, the sound carried on the wind. Between the weather and her laughter, he couldn't discern anything unusual.

'Shut the fuck up,' he snapped, but she continued her taunting.

'Do you hear them, Hee Haw? Do you hear that sound? It's the sound bloodhounds make when they're on a trail. They've got you now. They have your scent, and there's nothing you can do to escape. If you run, the dogs will give chase. They want you to run. They relish the hunt, the pursuit before dragging you down and mauling you, their teeth tearing out your throat. If they don't rip you apart—and you should wish they will, for it will be a swift end—the men will beat you to death with their cudgels. They're coming for you, Hee Haw. I've been listening while you slept. They're getting closer, encircling you. It's only a matter of time, Hee Haw. It's only a matter of time.'

'Shut up,' Hee Haw snapped, struggling to listen through the storm, anxious to hear any voices or barking, or anything which indicated danger.

Alice's laughter grew in intensity as he scrambled from the bed. Pulling on his underwear, he moved to the shack door and unbolted it. With caution, he opened it a crack and peeped outside. As he did, the wind tore it from his grasp, hurling it back on its hinges, the wood crashing against the outside wall.

Stepping out into the storm, he took a few paces towards the trees. The night was pitch black, an inky darkness smothering him. Above his head, the branches whipped around, driven into a frenzy by the turbulence, but aside from the wind, he couldn't hear anything.

He moved further into the trees, the cold, bitter squall biting at his skin. As he listened, a burning rage built inside him. Everything in his being screamed to go back inside, to punish the bitch, to teach her a lesson for her scorn, but a nagging doubt forced him to hesitate.

Could it be he'd missed something? Since snatching her, Alice's behaviour had been strange, but she was usually timid, almost apologetic. Why had she now switched to taunting him? It was a strange move, given her situation. Would she behave in such a confrontational manner unless convinced help was nearby? She *must* have heard something to give her hope, to empower her, fuelling her bravado and giving her the courage to fight back.

Holding his breath, he stood still, straining to hear any noises carried on the wind.

The gusts screamed through the treetops, branches creaking as the storm turned the woods into a maelstrom of chaos, but there were no sounds of dogs or people, or at least none he could hear. His skin prickled with goose-pimples, hairs standing up on his body. Maybe it was the night air's chill, or was the anxiety coursing through his body a warning? Danger could be lurking out there in the dark. He knew the woods: he certainly knew them better than any search-party would, but he couldn't be certain no one was out there. Something had triggered her new-found bravery.

His hand reached towards his belt, searching for his knife, before he remembered he wasn't dressed. Heading back to the shack, he struggled to pull the door closed against the force of the elements. As it slammed shut, the shack fell quiet, aside from the irritating giggle emerging from the box.

'The dogs knew you were out there,' she sniggered. 'They sensed your terror. They smelled your fear. They're stalking you, stealthily, silently, creeping ever closer, and you're trapped: nowhere to run, nowhere to hide.'

Her laughter increased in volume, as if she could sense the spikes of anxiety piercing his guts and wanted to mock his discomfort.

'There's no one out there, you fucking bitch,' he snarled, but she guffawed with disdain.

'I can hear the tremor of fear in your voice, Hee Haw,' she jeered. 'You're not certain it's safe, are you? You can feel the cold touch of doubt. The terror is only just beginning. Are the hounds on your trail, or was it a distant crow cawing, its aggressive screeches carried on the storm? Or was it a donkey, braying your name, calling out a warning to you, telling you to run and never look back? You don't know, Hee Haw; you just don't know.'

Her words ignited his anxiety, a catalyst for his fear. She was right: he didn't know, he wasn't sure. But there was one thing he could be certain of: right now, at this very moment, he was the one in control, not her. He would prove it to her ... and to himself.

Lowering the box, he flung the lid open and, without warning, lashed out, punching Alice in the face. He drove his fist into her jaw with all the force he could muster. He felt something crack, a bone or teeth. He didn't care. The thought of her pain only spurred him on. Struggling to control his rising anger, he punched again and again. Alice took every hit full in her face, the electrical flex tight on her neck, holding her in place so she couldn't evade the onslaught.

Continuing the assault, a searing pain shot through his hand, a sharp, burning twinge shooting up his arm. Pulling away, he looked at his fist. Embedded in the knuckle was a white object, small and shiny. It was one of her teeth.

'Cunt,' he muttered as he staggered to the sink. Running water over the injury, he washed away the blood before attempting to pull the tooth out. There was no way his large sausage-fingers could grip the enamel. Raising his hand to his mouth, he tried to bite onto the end of the shard, but only managed to push it further into the wound. It was hopeless. Whatever he tried would only make things worse. Tomorrow morning, he'd go up to the house and find a pair of tweezers or some pliers. Until then, he'd suffer.

Wrapping a grubby tea towel around his hand, he turned to face the box. Alice had fallen silent, the only sound her short and shallow breathing.

Edging closer, he looked inside.

Her face was splattered with blood, her lips split and dripping crimson droplets onto her white silk gown. Red blotches dotted her cheeks as the first stages of swelling became evident. One of her eyes was half-closed, the cheek below it already changing to a purple hue as the bruise spread.

'Not so mouthy now, are you?' he said, his tone chastising.

He wasn't to blame for hitting her. She'd brought it on herself. She'd taunted him, provoked him, and now she'd paid the price.

'See what you've done to yourself?' he asked, willing her to accept fault for her injuries, but she didn't respond.

'I said, see what you've done to yourself?'

She nodded, before looking up. Her bruised and battered face could not hide her spreading grin as she hissed, 'I bit you, Hee Haw. I bit you like the hounds which hunt you down. I bit you, and you'll bear the scar of shame for the rest of your days. I bit you, because I am the hound, and you are my prey.'

Then her head dropped, and she fell silent again.

Outside, the wind intensified, almost as a counterpoint to her silence. The storm howled, the roof of the shack echoing with the drumming of heavy rain drops, the rhythm increasing in volume and tempo as the skies opened, releasing a torrential downpour.

If there was anyone out there looking for him, they'd be soaked to the skin. Cold and wet through, disorientated in the darkness, they'd give up their search for the night. They'd go back to wherever it was they came from, kennel their hounds, and sit by a fire, drinking hot tea and waiting out the storm ... if they were out there.

Hee Haw closed the lid of the box and hauled it up off the floor, before returning to bed. Between the waxy, damp sheets, he shivered, curled in a ball, once more begging for sleep to take him under into the gloomy mist of dreamtime. The hammering of rain on the roof and the howling of the wind created a white noise, a lullaby helping him drift into the fuzzy haze.

As he hovered between wakefulness and sleep, the sounds of the storm coverged with a lilting, disjointed voice, childlike but also bearing the wisdom of eternity.

The sing-song incantation slithered from the suspended crate and wormed its way deep inside his head.

'Hark! Hark! The dogs do bark,
'The beggars have come to town.
'Some in rags, and some in tags,
'And one in a white silk gown.'

6: MEMORIES OF CHARLIE

The rising sun brought with it a calmness, the storm passing in the early hours. Hee Haw stretched out in his bed, exhausted by the emotional turmoil of the night. A grumbling ball of stress still bubbled in his guts, a gnawing tension which refused to dissipate. The miasma of discomfort hung in the air despite the quiet of the morning.

Turning onto his side, a searing pain shot up his arm, the throbbing agony reminding him of Alice's bite. Lifting his hand to examine the wound, he recoiled. From his wrist down, the limb was bloated and discoloured from the excessive swelling, his fingers resembling overstuffed sausages of putrid meat, ready to split. The knuckle in which Alice's tooth was buried had turned puffy and red, with a yellow-brown scab formed over the incision. Dark purple bruising spread across the other joints.

Lowering his hand back onto the stained mattress, Hee Haw winced. Every movement set off sharp pulses of distress, like fiery needles perforating his skin. Last night, the tip of the pearly enamel shard had been clearly visible, but now his swollen flesh seemed to have consumed the tooth.

His next steps were obvious: get up, clean the laceration as best he could, and wait for an opportunity to visit the house and remove the fragment. He'd need to dig inside the septic wound to locate it. The thought of doing so sent a shudder of revulsion through his body.

Glancing at the wooden crate suspended a few feet off the floor, he scowled. Fucking Alice: she'd pay for her histrionics before the day was out. He'd make her regret her mockery. This time he wouldn't shy away from hurting her. She had good reason to fear him before the previous night's madness, but now she should be twice as afraid. He might do what she suggested and cut off her eyelids. Fuck it; he'd go one step further and peel her whole face off. He'd wear it as a mask while he raped her.

She'd pay, but first, he needed to deal with the injury. Crawling from his bed, he dressed. It was a struggle to do so with one hand, but he managed to pull on his trousers and a shirt. Putting on socks proved to be too much of an effort, so he pushed his bare feet into his boots. Turning on the tap at the sink, he let the cold water trickle over the injury, washing away some of the crusty crap which had formed over the wound.

The numbing effect of the chilled water softened the sting of pain, and wrapping his hand in an old towel, he went outside.

The morning air was unusually crisp and clean, the storm having chased away any traces of humidity. The gentle breeze carried an odour of damp soil and pine needles, fresh and invigorating.

After filling his lungs a few times, Hee Haw turned and glanced towards the house. His father's bicycle leant against the wall. It wouldn't be long before the old bastard was on his way to work. Then he just needed to wait for his mother to head into the village, and he could deal with his hand.

If she saw the injury, she'd nag him to visit the doctor. Seeking medical help was the sort of stupid move which would draw attention from the authorities. He'd read enough about other murderers and kidnappers to recognise the mistakes which landed them in jail. He wouldn't repeat their errors. He was Hee Haw, for fuck's sake. He was the terrible monster the public would learn to fear.

Keeping out of sight, he squatted down with his back against the shack's wall and watched the house. After a while, his father came out. It took him an age to leave, fiddling with the bike, strapping his bag to the rack, going through the ritual of touching his pockets to make sure he had everything: keys, wallet, inhaler. Hee Haw knew he'd be saying the words aloud as he touched each item to reassure himself he hadn't forgotten anything. It was his ritual every time he left the house.

Once his father pedalled away and disappeared onto the road, Hee Haw settled back to await his mother's departure. Through the kitchen window, he could see her, washing up the morning's crockery, occasionally peering out towards the shack to see if he was coming in for breakfast. Eventually, she gave up and disappeared.

Her morning routine involved walking down to the village on some trivial errand to waste away her day, filling her monotonous life with mundane chores. The pain in his hand increased as he sat in his hiding place. Hopefully she'd leave soon. The last thing he needed was for her to have a bath or do her hair.

Time dragged as he waited. The throbbing in his hand intensified, the burning pain moving up his arm. In his head, he cursed Alice. He'd make her pay for her outburst.

How long would it take his mother to get ready? Why did old people take so long doing anything? They moaned about others wasting their last precious years on earth, but then took an eternity to do simple shit. She'd be in there, faffing around, moving crap from one place to another without any real reason. Why couldn't she just fuck off to the village? He only needed fifteen or twenty minutes in the bathroom to remove the tooth fragment, clean his hand with antiseptic, bandage it, and find some painkillers. That was all. Why didn't she hurry the fuck up?

The excruciating pain increased, an unpleasant prickling sensation pulsing up his arm to his elbow. The infection was spreading, septic poison creeping through his flesh, while his mother selfishly dithered. Maybe she needed to be taught a lesson too, once he'd dispensed his punishment to Alice.

Fixated on his injury, obsessed with the numbing ache, he nearly missed his mother waddling away from the house. As she disappeared down the lane, he crossed the garden to the back door. Fetching the spare key from under the flowerpot, he let himself in and headed straight to the bathroom.

Most of the things he needed were in the cabinet: antiseptic, cotton wool, gauze pads, plasters, and a pair of tweezers. The latter bore what looked like a dried crust of snot on one of the tips, a thick black hair protruding from the gunk. His dirty cunt of a mother had obviously been plucking her nasal hairs. Wiping them clean on his shirt, he cursed her filthy ways.

The only tablets in the bathroom cabinet were paracetamol. His father had some stronger medication, codeine phosphate, from a recent back injury. They'd be in his bedroom somewhere, but finding them would have to wait until he'd sorted his hand.

When Mother popped to the village shop, it took her a quarter of an hour to walk each way, plus she couldn't resist a gossip with anyone she met. That meant he had forty-five minutes at most to ensure he was gone before she returned.

Unwrapping the towel, the sight of his knuckle caused an involuntary yelp. The swelling had increased, the wound weeping a thick and sticky yellow pus. The skin surrounding the injury had turned an angry red and felt abnormally hot to the touch.

Drenching a ball of cotton wool with antiseptic, he cautiously dabbed at the wound. The liquid stung like a dozen angry wasps, the burning sensation sparking a wave of nausea deep in his guts. Cleaning away the scab and crusty muck, he still couldn't see the fragment of tooth in the puffy, tender flesh. He'd have to dig deep into the laceration to locate it.

Gripping the tweezers in his trembling hand, he pressed the tips into the hole, squeezing them together in an attempt to find the shard. As he pinched his raw flesh, a searing pain shot up his arm. Recoiling from the spike of agony, he emitted an involuntary shriek.

Taking the second attempt more slowly, he gently manoeuvred the tweezers into the cut. Squeezing the tips together, he hoped to feel a foreign object, but only pinched the inside of the injury again, and fresh blood filled the wound.

The tooth was in there. He could feel it when applying slight pressure with his fingertip, but getting a grip on it with the tweezers proved impossible. The only solution was to open the wound up, cutting into his hand so he could extract the chunk of enamel. What he needed was an old-fashioned razor blade, but his father used shitty plastic disposable ones. Staring at a pair of nail scissors in the cabinet, he wondered if the curved blades were sharp enough to snip through his flesh.

Teeth gritted, he winced as the curved metal dug deeper into the septic laceration, until he felt the blade touch the enamel shard. Holding his breath, he gently squeezed, applying pressure until the blades pinched his skin. With his face screwed up, ready for the explosion of pain, he forced the scissors closed, cutting through his flesh.

An anguished howl echoed off the tiled walls as warm blood flowed over his hand and dripped into the bathroom sink. Pushing the blades deeper, he tried to lever out the fragment. As he worked the scissors into the swollen knuckle, tears welled up in his eyes and tumbled down his cheeks.

A steady stream of blood ran from the wound, splashing on the white porcelain as he prised at the tooth buried deep inside his gore-smeared hand. Unable to lever it out, he dropped the nail scissors and picked up the tweezers. Without hesitation, he pushed the tips into the wound, and after some manoeuvring, finally managed to get a purchase on the end of the tooth.

The pain was searing as he carefully wiggled the sliver to loosen it. Acrid saliva filled his mouth as a rising tide of bile filled his gullet. Taking a deep breath, with one final jerk, he yanked it free, letting it drop into the basin and as he doubled over and dry-heaved a few times.

Grabbing a wad of gauze, he applied pressure to the wound, waiting for the cut to congeal. As his head stopped spinning, he glanced at what he'd pulled from his knuckle. It wasn't a fragment; it was a whole fucking tooth, root and all. Pointed and curved like a tiny sabre, the fang had a familiar look.

Two or maybe three years ago, he'd been out in the woods when a little dog appeared. It was one of those small breeds which old people favour as pets. Expecting it to run off back to its owner, he'd ignored it, but the dog followed him, seemingly happy with his company. After an hour or more, he realised it wasn't going to leave. It wore a collar, but no tag, so Hee Haw named him Charlie. Threading a length of twine through the collar, he led his new pet back to the shack.

Food, warmth and company kept the mutt happy for a few days, but then things changed. Out for a walk one afternoon, they got close to the edge of the village, and suddenly Charlie became animated. Straining against the twine leash, he recognised where he was and wanted to run off, no doubt to wherever he lived. Despite all the love he'd shown Charlie, the dog was ready to abandon him without a care.

Squatting down, Hee Haw could sense the animal's excitement. Tenderly, he wrapped his hands around Charlie's throat and squeezed, choking the life out of his ungrateful friend.

He threw the dog's body in a dried-up stream bed, covering it with sticks and leaves and moss. Throughout the summer, every time he passed by, he checked on Charlie to see how the dog was doing. At first, the carcass swelled, its belly becoming as tight as a drum. The cadaver remained intact for longer than he expected, but once the beast's stomach ruptured, it quickly decayed. The body rotted away, and Hee Haw forgot about Charlie, but as autumn approached, he found himself back at the dry stream bed. Curiosity got the better of him, and he checked on his short-lived friend. All that remained was the animal's skeleton.

Hee Haw took the skull back to the shack and put it on a shelf next to his bed. That was where he'd seen the hooked fang before.

Standing in the bathroom, his hand still dripping blood onto the white porcelain, he stared at the tooth he'd dug out of his knuckle.

It was a dog's tooth.

7: EXTRACTION POINT

With his hand bandaged, Colin headed for the garage in search of tools. One benefit of his father's anal obsession with everything having a clearly demarked place was things were easy to find. Everything was where it ought to be. Unlike normal people who lived in various states of organised and semi-organised chaos, his father went to great pains to make his world as orderly as possible. Printed labels adorned the shelves, and even the boxes stacked on them were clearly marked. In a large wooden cabinet bearing an ornately calligraphed sign designating it for 'hand tools', he found what he needed.

Selecting a pair of long-nosed pliers, he turned them over a few times, considering their size. They would be ideal for reaching into Alice's mouth to grip her teeth. They'd also allow enough room for manoeuvre if he needed to wiggle a tooth to make it loose. Having never detoothed a child, he didn't know how much force would be needed to pull them free from her jawbone.

Next, he picked up a pair of combination pliers. Sturdy and heavy-duty, they'd be ideal to yank the teeth out once loosened. He assumed her molars and pre-molars would need a fair degree of leverage during extraction.

One thing was certain: he'd find out if she had dog's teeth, even if it meant pulling out every single one. It would be a punishment for her bad attitude, ensuring she understood he was in control. She needed to know she couldn't pull the sort of stunt she had the previous night and get away with it.

With the tools gathered, Colin took one last look around the garage. It was critical he didn't need to come back, not if his mother or father were home.

Spotting an old wooden tea chest with the word 'Gardening' stencilled on the side, he browsed the selection of implements. Pulling out a machete, he swung it in the air, feeling its balance in his hand. Satisfied, he headed back to the house and into the kitchen. After making a cheese and pickle sandwich, he went outside, locked the back door, and returned the key to its hiding place.

Eating the sandwich, he strode to the shack. Today would be the day he regained control. He wouldn't tolerate her shit, not anymore. Today she'd suffer, and he'd live out his fantasies. Alice wouldn't know what hit her. There would be no warning; he'd just start pulling out her fucking teeth. Then, when he'd extracted every last one of them, the real brutality would begin.

Letting himself into the shack, a sensation of dread washed over him. Something didn't feel right. He couldn't put his finger on it, but panic bubbled inside his belly as he glanced around. With a breath caught in his throat, he struggled to comprehend what he saw. The box was on the ground, lowered down, and the lid was open.

Dropping the pliers and brandishing the machete, he crept towards it, his heart hammering out a frenzied rhythm on his rib cage.

Peeping inside, he let out an agonised moan. The crate was empty.

In a split second, the shack felt cold, freezing, his skin burning with the blistering chill. The room span, a slow but jilting rotation which made him nauseous. A high-pitched whine echoed in his head, the sound of confusion and panic.

Where the fuck was Alice?

How had she escaped? Her hands and feet were tied, her neck lashed to the side of the crate, and the fucking thing had been suspended off the floor. He'd only been in the house long enough to pull the tooth out of his hand and grab a few tools. How could she undo her bonds, climb out, and escape in that short time?

Hee Haw froze, his last thought echoing in his head. If she managed to untie her hands and feet, and climbed out of the crate, why did she then lower it to the ground? The second she freed herself, she would have run into the woods and kept on running until she found someone to help her. The only reason to lower the box was ...

Hee Haw leaned over and puked, his stomach spasming as it voided the remnants of the cheese and pickle sandwich, along with strings of sticky bile, onto the floor.

Inside his head, the thought resounded, an echoing scream of terror. The only reason for the box to be lowered was if *someone else* had freed Alice.

Hee Haw clutched the side of the crate and peered inside again. The ropes and electrical flex were missing. The only signs Alice had ever been there were a sticky sludge of piss and shit on the base, a few smears of dried blood on the wooden slats, and a couple of long, black hairs stuck to the lid.

Whoever freed her was out there, in the woods, trying to get away. They'd be desperate to raise the alarm and bring the mob after him. He couldn't waste any time. Every second he thought about things was another second they had to escape. He had to find them, to kill her rescuer, and bring Alice back.

Gripping the machete, Hee Haw headed outside.

Where would they go? Where would they run? The obvious place had to be the village. There were other dwellings nearby, but without knowing the area, they were difficult to find ... unless her rescuer was a local. But who?

No one ever called at the house. The villagers didn't like his father, and only tolerated his mother because she forced herself upon people, oblivious to their disdain. For as long as he could remember, no one had ever called to see him, so who was it? It could only be a random passer-by, a stranger who happened on the shack, but why would they walk past the house to visit his crumbling abode? It made no sense, unless they'd got lost in the woods and stumbled on the shack, not realising there was a house further up the path.

Setting off at a run, Hee Haw wove through the trees, his eyes flicking from side to side, scanning the horizon. Nothing moved. He'd become accustomed to spotting anything amongst the boughs: small animals, birds, even changes to the flora. These were his woods, and he held an advantage over anyone who tried to evade him.

As he raced on, he played through the possible scenarios in his head. First, he'd have to disable the rescuer. It would probably be an adult, hopefully unarmed. The best-case scenario was they'd freeze as soon as they saw the machete. The worst-case was he'd have to fight them.

He hadn't been involved in a physical confrontation since he was a child, when the local bullies dragged him behind the cricket pavilion and beat him black and blue for grassing when they stole cider from the village shop. After that, he'd become introverted, avoiding other children. Now, things were different. He'd have to fight to ensure whoever had Alice didn't contact the police.

Hacking someone down couldn't be difficult. He'd seen some of the thick idiots arrested for knife and axe crimes on the news. If they could do it, he could too. One swing, one lunge, and it would take a brave person to come back for more. Then he'd face a more critical decision: what to do with them. He could drag Alice back to the shack, but an injured adult would represent a greater risk. Killing them was the only option.

He'd cross that bridge when he needed to. For now, it was imperative he focused on the search. They were out there, somewhere, frightened and hiding in the woods; they had to be.

Reaching the treeline, he hovered in the shadows, scanning the horizon. There was no sign of movement anywhere on the open fields, and the village beyond was blanketed with its usual somnolence. If anyone had arrived with a rescued abductee, there didn't seem to be much interest. Nothing ever happened in the area, so a stranger claiming to have released a captive girl would fire up the local busybodies, but aside from a dog limping down the main street, there was no other activity.

Turning, Hee Haw ducked back into the trees. Gripping the machete, ready to strike if anyone surprised him, he moved with stealth. Heading away from his shack, he went towards a small farm further along the road. The old farmer wasn't a sociable sort. If anything, he was a nasty cunt, so if the stranger had taken Alice there, a small chance existed they wouldn't have found the help they wanted.

All around, the woodland was still, as if even the birds and animals knew today was not the day to cross Hee Haw. Fear and anxiety still bubbled in his guts, but alongside the negative emotions was a growing sense of determination. This would be a critical confrontation, one which determined the rest of his life. If he killed the stranger, there was a chance he'd remain free, but if he didn't, it was certain he'd spend the rest of his life behind bars. He'd be a hated man, a target for the other prisoners. No one liked a child molester. He'd have no rest until they took his life, or he took his own.

The trees thinned out as he approached the farm, the air filled with a whirring, mechanical cacophony. An old tractor crawled its way across the horizon, ploughing up the soil. A rush of relief washed over Hee Haw. If the rescuer had bought Alice here, the farmer would be contacting the authorities, not working the fields. Unless they'd gone to the farmhouse.

Hee Haw's anxiety spiked once more as he skirted the treeline, creeping towards the house, but he couldn't see anyone. As soon as he broke cover, the farmer's dog reacted, a crescendo of barks cutting through the stillness. The dog had been placid until it spotted him, so it was unlikely anyone else was nearby.

'Fuck it,' Hee Haw muttered to himself, his frustration bubbling over.

Moving back into the woods, he paused to think. Whoever had freed Alice hadn't taken her to the village nor to the farm. If they had local knowledge, those were the two obvious places. The only other possibility was they'd just run, blindly meandering through the woods. They could be anywhere, and the chances of finding them diminished with every passing minute.

The bravado which drove Hee Haw to contemplate murdering Alice's rescuer deserted him, the vacuum being filled with the fear of arrest. The thought of spending the rest of his life caged, of being bullied, tormented, and tortured, terrified him.

He had no other option but to flee, to get as far away as he could. First, he'd need to destroy anything which gave a clue Alice had been there. If there was no evidence, they might not give credibility to the claims of a young girl who was, quite clearly, not right in the head.

Striding with purpose, no longer worried about being seen, Hee Haw hurried back towards his home. He needed to eliminate any evidence and be gone as quickly as he could. If Mother wasn't back from the village, he'd raid the house for money and anything of use in his flight. If she had returned, then ... he'd still need to do it, even if it meant using force against her.

Breaking through the trees into the garden, Hee Haw stopped dead in his tracks, another pulse of nausea forcing him to dry heave.

The door of the shack was open.

He never left it open. Even in his earlier blind panic, he'd locked it. He was sure he did. Feeling in his pocket, he touched the key. He *had* locked it.

Holding the machete before him in a trembling hand, he inched towards the open door. From outside, looking in, all he could see was darkness, the inky blackness swallowing whatever awaited him. Every nerve in his body tingled as he edged closer.

Taking a deep breath, and mentally uttering a prayer for his survival, Hee Haw dashed into the gloom.

The shack was empty. In the middle of the room the wooden crate hung, suspended off the floor, its lid closed. Creeping closer, he listened.

From inside, he could hear soft, shallow breathing.

With trembling fingers, he untied the rope and lowered the box. His heart hammered out a frenzied rhythm, so intense he could feel the veins in his temples expand and contract.

Raising the blade, ready to strike, he flipped the lid open with his other hand.

From inside the box, the battered face of Alice looked up at him.

Then she smiled, a knowing smile which sent a chill through his being, right to his very core.

8: FATHER'S DAY

Hee Haw didn't speak as he ripped the flex from
Alice's neck and manhandled her out of the box.
Pushing her down, he drove his fist into her belly
and she flopped like a fish out of water. Curled on
the floor, an agonised groan escaped her lips as he
took hold of her stained silk gown and, with three or
four jerks, tore it from her body. Lying naked,
trembling, she looked frail and weak, her body
almost skeletal and dotted with yellowing bruises.

Resting the machete blade on her slender neck,
he squatted down, his snarl clearly displaying his
displeasure.

'You know what you did, you snotty little cunt,'
he hissed, 'and now you're going to pay. It's time
you understood who's in charge around here.'

Alice closed her eyes, her whole body tense as if
awaiting execution.

'Don't move,' he ordered, before scrambling
across the floor and grabbing the pliers.

Once back at her side, he brandished the long-
nosed pair. Realising he'd have to put down the
machete to force her mouth open, he dropped the
blade and positioned himself so his knee pressed
against her neck. Shifting his body weight, he used his
bulk to pin her down. Despite struggling to breathe,

she didn't resist, accepting the discomfort without so much as a whimper. When he placed his hand on her jaw and pulled it open, she willingly complied.

Peering inside her mouth, Hee Haw felt uneasy. He didn't see the expected curved fangs of a dog. Her teeth looked like normal children's teeth, small and shining with the pearlescence of unblemished enamel.

Unsure what to do, he hesitated, but Alice opened her eyes. She didn't flinch at the sight of the pliers hovering close to her mouth. Her eyes moved from the tool to Hee Haw's face, and she nodded, the slightest of movements encouraging him to do what he needed to do.

Gripping a front tooth, he tried to pull it free, but it was firmly lodged in her jaw. Grunting with the exertion, he pushed it forwards and backwards, the range of movement increasing as the root loosened in the bone. A ring of crimson gore appeared around the base as blood oozed from her gum.

Alice didn't make a sound. She kept her mouth open wide, allowing him access as he jerked and pulled until the tooth moved freely. Then, switching to the combination pliers, he gave it a hefty yank, and it came free.

The tooth was small but perfect, a blade-like incisor of brilliant white with a bloody root. Compared to the fang which had been lodged in his fist, it was clearly human.

'What the fuck?' he muttered.

'What's the matter?' Alice lisped, her speech affected by the extraction.

'It's a fucking human tooth,' Hee Haw said, more to himself than to her.

'What did you expect; a dog's tooth?'

She smiled as her words percolated in his head. Again, it was that knowing smirk which stung like a barb of mockery. Hee Haw felt his guts turn over as she gazed at him, her grin tinged with pity.

'Why did you say that?' he snapped.

'Say what?' she asked, her face a picture of innocence.

'Why say a dog's tooth? Why not another animal?'

Alice shrugged.

'I don't know. I suppose because dogs are commonplace. There are dogs everywhere. It would have been weird if I'd said a panda's tooth, or an ocelot's tooth, but a dog's tooth sounded right. Were you thinking of a dog's tooth too?'

Hee Haw struggled to suppress the uneasy feeling invading his thoughts. Something wasn't right, and the awkward blazing sensation in every nerve of his body screamed in alarm.

'Shut up,' he hissed, 'or I'll rip out every single one of your fucking teeth.'

Alice's gaze dropped, her eyes fixed on the floor, but she slowly opened her mouth to allow him to continue. In that moment, deep inside his bubbling anxiety, he knew she was laughing at him.

The ridicule stung like a lash tearing welts in his consciousness. How dare she taunt him. He was in control, not her. As the newfound rage pulsed through his body, Hee Haw pushed the pliers in and caught hold of another tooth. He started to shake it, loosening the root, when suddenly the door to the shack opened and his father marched in.

'Colin,' he said sternly, 'I've just got home and popped into the garage, and someone has moved my...'

The chastising words died in his throat as he spotted Alice, her mouth bleeding as she laid naked on the floor, pinned down by his son. The sight deflated him, his pomposity and indignation immediately disappearing.

'Oh no; no, no, no,' he stammered. 'What the fuck have you done now? Who is she, and what's going on?'

Hee Haw froze, staring back at his father. The moment seemed to stretch into infinity, time slowing as the two faced each other.

Dropping the bloodied pliers, Hee Haw snatched up the machete.

'Let her go, Colin,' his father said, his voice calm and steady, but as he held out his arms and beckoned to Alice, his hands shook.

'Fuck off, you bastard,' Hee Haw hissed, brandishing the weapon above Alice's neck. 'Fuck off right now, or I'll chop her bastarding head off.'

'Don't do anything stupid, Colin,' his father said, a slight tremor creeping into his tone. 'We can work this out. There's no need for anyone to get hurt.'

'I'm not bluffing; I'll do it,' Hee Haw screamed. 'I'll fucking kill her.'

His father took a few steps backwards as a placatory gesture, but never broke the gaze between himself and his son.

'Calm down, Colin. Don't do anything rash. There's got to be a better solution than this. You don't want to be killing anyone. Whatever is happening, I'm sure ... I'm sure we can resolve it. The first thing, the most important thing, is to let the little girl go. Look at her; she's terrified.'

Hee Haw glanced at Alice. She didn't look terrified, not to him. Was she grinning? He could see a smirk lingering on the edges of her bloodied lips.

'I can't let her go,' Hee Haw muttered. 'Not now. It's too late.'

'You can,' his father said softly, a genuine hint of empathy in his voice.

Did the fucker care? After all these years of hostility, did he actually give a damn?

'Let her go. Let me take her inside to Mother, and then we can decide how we're going to put things right.'

The moment felt timeless, suspended in nothingness, as Hee Haw's head burbled with indecision. Whatever he did, whichever outcome he decided on, would be permanent. There was no going back, whether he released Alice or killed her.

This was it. This was the end. Whichever path he chose was irrelevant; his father wouldn't ignore what he'd seen. He couldn't just release Alice and walk away. Not now.

'Save me,' Alice gasped, and his father edged forwards, retaking the steps he'd previously retreated.

'Stay back or I'll cut her fucking head off,' Hee Haw snarled, raising the machete.

'No, you won't, Colin,' his father said. 'You're not an evil person. You're a good boy, a bit misguided and lost in the world, maybe, but you're not bad.'

'I am,' Hee Haw whispered, as if trying to convince himself. 'I'm evil down to my core. I am Hee Haw, and Hee Haw is evil.'

'But you're not Hee Haw, you're Colin,' his father said, his tone caring and kind, 'and Colin isn't evil.'

'Save me,' Alice cried, a little more forcefully. 'Please. He raped me.'

Hee Haw shuddered. Why did she say that? He hadn't raped her. He wanted to, he intended to, he'd fantasised about it, but he hadn't done it. Not yet.

'I didn't rape you,' he muttered to Alice, but his eyes remained locked on his father, trying to assess his next move.

'Please help me,' Alice sobbed. 'He raped me and beat me and forced me to do vile things.'

'I fucking didn't,' Hee Haw snapped, before remembering he did beat her after she bit him. But the other things? He hadn't done them. If anything, he'd tried to be nice.

'I didn't rape you,' he said again, shaking his head.

'Help me,' Alice screamed. 'Hee Haw, help me and kill him. He raped me.'

'*What?*' Hee Haw asked, confused by her accusations.

'He raped me, Hee Haw,' Alice screamed, her trembling hand pointing at his father. 'That man there; he raped me. Save me from him.'

Hee Haw glanced at Alice. For the first time since he'd snatched her, she looked petrified, not of him, but of his father.

'What are you saying, that my father raped you?'

'Yes,' she howled. 'Save me from him.'

'Look here young lady,' his father said, the soft tone of his voice replaced with indignation. 'I don't know what the fuck is going on, but I think it's best if I call the police.'

'Kill him, Hee Haw,' Alice shouted, her pleas becoming more hysterical. 'Slay the monster and save me.'

Raising the machete, Hee Haw pointed at his father and asked, 'What did you do?'

'I didn't do anything,' his father replied, spitting the words out in anger. 'Whatever's going on here is wrong, and unless you get a grip on yourselves and do the right thing, you'll both be going to prison for a long, long time.'

Hee Haw looked down at Alice, her face contorted in fear.

'When did he rape you?' he asked.

'When I was little,' Alice said, her screams fading to a whisper as her lips trembled. 'He would come to me at night and force me to do bad things. He would hurt me and torture me and tell me I'd brought it all on myself. He said he had a right to do it, because—'

'She's lying,' his father spat.

'Because what?' Hee Haw asked.

Alice sobbed, shaking with emotion, her whole body wracked with misery as tears tumbled down her face.

'Because what?' Hee Haw repeated, shouting the question at the cowering girl.

'Because ... he's my father,' she blubbed.

'Bullshit,' the old man snapped. 'I don't know the girl; I've never seen her before in my life. I'm not standing for this, for fuck's sake. I come in here and find you wrestling a naked girl who's ... well, who's clearly too young to be alone with you. Plus, she's bleeding. But then the pair of you turn on me, accusing me of something unspeakable. I'll be honest, Colin, I *am* going to call the police, and I hope they lock you up and throw away the fucking key. As for her, she needs psychiatric help.'

'You see,' Alice whispered, conspiratorially. 'He abandoned me, just like he's abandoning you. Kill him, Hee Haw. Kill the cunt.'

'That's enough, young lady,' his father said, his voice dripping with contempt. 'I didn't abandon Colin. He lives in my fucking back garden. I didn't abandon him; he abandoned reality. Everything that happens to him is his own fault. He likes to play the victim, but he's a spoilt brat who's incapable of standing on his own two feet. He's a failure, a loser, and I'm ashamed to think I brought him into the world.'

Hee Haw rose.

'Kill him, Hee Haw,' Alice hissed. 'He abused me, and he abused you.'

Hee Haw took a step towards his father, brandishing the machete.

'Enough is enough,' his father snapped, his patience finally eroded. 'Put that thing down and come up to the house with me. This ends right now.'

'Too right, old man,' Hee Haw replied. 'It does end now.'

'Colin, I'm warning you,' his father said, standing his ground.

'I'm not Colin; I'm Hee Haw.'

'Oh, for fuck's sake, Colin; grow up.'

Hee Haw raised the machete. His father did not flinch. He did not flinch as the weapon hovered in the air. He did not flinch as Hee Haw swung it downwards in an arc. He did not flinch as the honed metal blade cut into his neck, cleaving his flesh in two and removing his head from its usual position atop his shoulders.

A spray of hot crimson blood hung in the air like a fine mist of the tiniest rubies, sparkling in the afternoon sun. Hee Haw raised the blade again and hacked downward at the toppling body of his father. He slashed and sliced at the fallen man, a frenzied attack fuelled by years of hatred and resentment and boiling rage. Inside his head, Alice's shrill, screaming voice ricocheted amongst his turbulent emotions.

'Kill him, Hee Haw. Kill him. He abused me, and he abused you. Kill our father, who art in heaven, hallowed be his name.'

9: HANGED FOR A SHEEP

Hee Haw gasped, unable to suck in air. His chest tightened, and the more he tried to inhale, the harder it became to fill his lungs. Light-headed and dizzy, the interior of the shack swirled and twisted, becoming almost elastic in the chaos of the moment. Sweat rolled off his body as the day became unbearably humid, the air taking on a soup-like quality, hot and steamy and impossible to breathe. It felt surreal, like a bad dream, as he knelt beside the mutilated body of his father.

Pure silence enveloped him, as if all sound had been sucked out of the world. The quietness was oppressive, almost deafening, and he battled against the rising swell of confusion, trying to make sense of the decapitated cadaver which lay before him.

He still gripped the handle of machete, his fist so tense the skin on his knuckles was white, his hand trembling due to the force with which he clutched the weapon. Everything in his being wanted to throw it aside, to hurl it as far from him as he possibly could, but equally the compulsion to not let go, to hang on to it, was overwhelming.

He'd never killed before. Well, there'd been Charlie, and he'd shot a few rats when the compost heap became overrun with vermin, but he'd never ended a person's life. He'd fantasised about it, dreamed of it, but in his head the victims had always been young girls. Now, he'd actually taken a life, and it had been his father's.

The otherworldliness of the corpse on the floor was added to by the situation. It didn't seem real that this man, the bastard who'd sired him, had also created Alice. What were the odds of snatching his half-sister in the woods that day? Coincidences didn't come bigger than that, unless...

A shiver of icy tension crept over Hee Haw's scalp. Did it explain why no one was out searching for Alice? Did her own father, his father, have more to lose if she'd been reported missing and someone actually found her? Was she running from him, trying to escape a rapist, and rather than offering her the salvation she sought, he'd brought her back to the very place she was running from? The old man wouldn't have dared inform the authorities about his bastard daughter. He'd be too busy trying to cover his tracks. It added up, but it still made no sense.

The old man cheating on Mother wasn't beyond the realms of possibility, but the odds on his father's runaway daughter being kidnapped by her own half-brother were unthinkable. If Alice really was his father's child, where had she been all her life, and why had she turned up in the woods a few days ago?

'What I don't understand is where you've been,' Hee Haw muttered.

The silence felt uneasy, uncomfortable. Turning to face Alice, to confront her with his doubts, he realised he was alone.

An electric surge of panic cut through the confusion, jolting him awake. Where the fuck had she gone? He'd been transfixed by his dead father, sucked into the chaos of the situation. While he'd been drowning in the madness of the moment, she'd simply got up and walked away without him noticing.

Using the machete to lever himself upright, he stood for a moment on shaking legs, waiting for his head to stop spinning and his balance to return. Clutching the weapon, unsure where she'd be or what she'd be doing, he staggered outside.

Alice stood on the lawn, naked, her body daubed with swirls of drying blood. It couldn't have all come from the tooth he'd pulled out. She'd clearly smeared herself with the gore puddled around the old man's butchered body. She stared at the house, and from the kitchen window, framed between the folds of net curtains, his mother stared back, eyebrows raised and mouth hanging open. Her face portrayed a mixture of confusion and fear, but as she saw her son emerge, it transformed into anger. Then she disappeared.

Before Hee Haw could reach Alice, the back door of the house burst open. With a determined stride, his mother marched towards him, her usual brow-beaten demeanour replaced with something approaching rage.

'Colin, what do you think you're doing? Who in the name of hell is this ... this girl? I doubt she's old enough to be out on her own, let alone with you, and why is she naked?'

'Don't you recognise her?' Hee Haw asked with sarcasm. 'Surely you know who she is? Did you birth her, or was it Father's fancy woman who spat her out into the world?'

'What are you talking about?' his mother snapped, her face creased with disapproval.

'She, this girl, is the fruit of my father's loins,' Hee Haw said with defiance. 'He's far from the perfect husband, eh? But I'm guessing you knew about his secret lovechild. I bet you kept the bastard's dirty secret, just to make certain you had an easy ride. Was that the deal: you ignored his indiscretions in exchange for a lazy life?'

'Don't talk such nonsense, Colin.'

She barked at him, her words stinging. Her tongue was barbed, as it had been years ago when he was still at school. Her displeasure at the naughty boy cut deep.

'It's true,' Hee Haw replied, a grin of smug satisfaction on his face. 'Father not only had a bastard child, but he raped her too.'

His mother stopped her march, frozen for a moment, as if someone had delivered a hefty slap to her scowling face.

'Impossible,' she spat. 'For starters, your father had a vasectomy after you were born. Let's also not forget he's been impotent for the last twenty years. So, please, explain to me how your lies have any basis in reality. I don't appreciate whatever idiocy you're up to. Where's your father? He won't be happy when I tell him about your behaviour.'

Mother's words echoed in Hee Haw's head, tipping the situation into a whirl of confusion. His father couldn't have had a vasectomy. He couldn't be impotent. It didn't make any sense, because that would mean...

'About your husband,' Alice said, her cheery voice interrupting Hee Haw's cataclysmic thoughts. 'He sent me to fetch you. I'm afraid he's had an accident.'

'Who is she, Colin, and why is she covered with blood?' Mother whined, her stress beginning to show.

Hee Haw shrugged and muttered, 'I think her tooth fell out.'

'Colin, what have you done? What's happened to Daddy?'

His mother teetered on the verge of hysteria. Everything was spiralling out of control.

'Follow me,' Alice said calmly, turning and heading towards the shack. Walking past Hee Haw, she flashed him that smile, the knowing grin. Chaos overwhelmed him and his world crumbled, but the little bitch was enjoying herself. The more she whipped up the insanity, the wider her smile became. Had she fabricated her claim his father was also hers? Was the rape another lie? As the questions echoed in his mind, he already knew the answers.

His mother began hyperventilating as she drew closer to her husband's remains, as if she sensed the reality of his death. A loud sob broke free from her rouged maw, her legs buckling as the yawning doorway came into sight, the darkness sucking her towards the carnage hidden within.

Hee Haw followed, brandishing the machete as if expecting an attack. He knew what was coming, the emotional meltdown which would unfold. His mother's mental state was on a rollercoaster ride from confusion, through anger, to devastation, and her mind was about to completely dissolve. There would be an inevitable wallow in the abject misery of the moment before she twisted her grief into self-pity. She wouldn't wail for the demise of her husband, but for herself. It was always about her.

As she disappeared into the gloom, her scream, a shriek of despair and shock, shattered the afternoon. Her anguish was futile, Hee Haw thought. All the histrionic outbursts in the world weren't about to bring the old bastard back to life.

By the time he got inside the shack, his mother was on the floor, grabbing at the mangled mess of meat which used to be his father. Her whole body shook as she sobbed while trying to lift the body, as if willing it to get up and resume living.

'Calm down, please,' Hee Haw begged. 'I had to kill him after what he'd done.'

His mother stopped sobbing, her body trembling more with rage than misery. Turning her blood-smeared face towards him, she hissed, 'Colin, what have you done? I hope you burn in Hell.'

'He cheated on you, Mum. She's his illegitimate child, and he raped her, for fuck's sake. You can't blame me.'

'You're mentally ill,' his mother hissed. 'You're evil.'

Turning to Alice, Hee Haw pleaded, 'Tell her. Tell her what you told me. Tell her what he did to you.'

'You know you're going to have to kill her too,' Alice said to Hee Haw, ignoring his prompting. 'She won't let you get away with this. She won't keep quiet. You'll be hauled off to jail, beaten and sodomised by the other prisoners, and every day of your life will be unending misery, all because of her. You've got no choice; you have to kill the bitch.'

Once more, his mother's demeanour changed, her focus switching to self-preservation.

'Don't hurt me, Colin,' she whined. 'This is a mess, but I'm the only person who can help you. Please don't kill me.'

'You truly are a wheedling cunt,' Hee Haw spat, a wave of contempt flooding through his belly. All those times she'd sat by in silence while his bastard father talked down to him, and only now, on finding herself at the wrong end of his machete, did she want to be his friend.

Before he could voice his thoughts, Alice interjected.

'Look at her,' she said coldly. 'A mother's instinct should be to protect her children, but all she cares about is herself. She'll say and do anything to save her own precious hide, but trust me on this: the first moment an opportunity arises, she'll hand you over to the mob. If you don't kill her, it's just a matter of time until she betrays you.'

'I can't kill my own mother,' Hee Haw muttered.

'Yes, you can,' Alice said, her words becoming more emotional. 'You've already rid the world of your father, so what difference does it make if you kill her too? May as well be hanged for a sheep as a lamb.'

'Colin, I don't know who she is, but she's trouble,' his mother said, her tone pleading. 'Don't hurt me and maybe we can...'

Her words trailed off, her lips trembling, as her eyes beseeched him to show mercy.

'We can what?' Hee Haw asked.

His mother looked away, as if ashamed of what she was about to say. It was a trait of hers, a way to appear vulnerable just before suggesting something horrendous.

'We could what?' Hee Haw repeated, his demand more forceful.

'We could ... blame her for Daddy's murder,' his mother muttered.

Brandishing the machete in his shaking hand, Hee Haw glanced at Alice, then back at his mother. Even if they both swore Alice had killed his father, would anyone believe them? Would anyone really believe a young girl had hacked a grown man limb from limb? She hardly had enough strength to lift the machete.

Spotting Hee Haw's indecision, his mother increased her attempts at coercion.

'She's right when she says they'll make your life a misery in prison, and you wouldn't survive, but the answer isn't to kill me. If anything, I'm the only one who can help you. I'm your mother, after all, but who is she? I doubt you know anything about her. I mean, how did she even get here?'

'She came looking for her father,' Hee Haw snarled. 'Her father, who raped her. Remember?'

'Please, Colin, listen to me,' his mother begged. 'I've already explained Daddy couldn't be her father, nor would he have raped anyone, let alone a little girl. Do you really think I'd turn a blind eye if I thought Daddy was raping a child?'

'Don't listen to her lies,' Alice said, her tone now carrying a sense of urgency. 'You know what he did to me, and she stood by. She let him mock and abuse you and never spoke up to protect you. Are you a mummy's boy, doing whatever that manipulative bitch tells you? Are you hanging onto her apron strings, or are you a man? Show her what Daddy did to me. See how she likes it. Beat her and strip her naked and rape her, and show no emotion while you do it, just like your stone-hearted father. You are Hee Haw, and Hee Haw dispenses justice to the morally repugnant. Show her how it feels.'

'I am Hee Haw,' Hee Haw declared, his words a guttural battle cry.

Undoing his belt, he let his trousers drop to the floor. His mother screamed, a cacophony of pleas and prayers and beseechments as he knelt beside her, his bloodied hands tearing at her dress and underwear, exposing her sagging breasts and fat belly and wiry bush of pubic hair.

'Show her how it feels,' Alice barked, her words almost a snarl. 'Let her understand how I felt: the

84

shame and pain, the self-loathing, the same disgust you felt when she stood by and let your father crush your spirit. Show her the depth of your contempt, Hee Haw. Make her understand the error of her ways.'

Looking down at his mother, he gazed into her eyes. They were pools of the blackest black, an all-consuming darkness in which her unbridled fears resided. He saw her terror, her pain, her inescapable shame. He saw her weakness and uncertainty, her vulnerability, her self-loathing and her soul-crushing doubt.

Raping her wasn't necessary. She had nothing left.

Raising the machete, he brought the blade down, splitting her head like a watermelon.

10: TOGETHER BOUND

Hee Haw sat between the bodies of his mother and father, knees pulled up, head down. Swaying, humming, he would have given anything to be a child again, to be protected and cared for and away from the insanity. Inside his head, a cauldron of chaos raged. How had things come to this?

He'd known Alice's claims were untrue. His father was a bastard, and probably would have embraced infidelity if he ever found another woman who'd look at him twice, but he lacked the depth of depravity to rape anyone, let alone a child. Even as he'd hacked and slashed at the dead meat which once brought him into the world, he knew the old fucker wasn't her father, but her words had been enough to push him into action.

It had been enough.

'Why did you say those things about...?'

There was no need to finish the question. They both knew what he was asking.

Alice shrugged.

'I suppose I just wanted you to kill him,' she said with a sweet innocence, as if discussing her favourite food or which animals she liked to pet.

'Why would you want that?' Hee Haw asked, desperate for an answer.

'It was for the best,' Alice said with a smile. 'You needed to do it. You needed to be free, to stand on your own two feet, to be your own man, and your father held you back. Killing him was your rebirth, a moment of defiance and liberation. You freed yourself from his clutches. He oppressed you, and now you're unshackled.'

Hee Haw nodded and, drifting into silence, mulled over her words. His father had been a pain in the arse, a nuisance, but could he be described as an oppressor? Did he really represent that much of a threat? It was true he'd lived a miserable life, and reflected that misery onto others, but did he deserve to be hacked to death by his own son? Was a brutal death the price of being unhappy?

While it may not have been justified, killing the old man did have its benefits. Hee Haw had no doubt he would have informed the police about Alice. He would have thought it the right thing to do. Protecting his son wouldn't have entered his head.

'I can see killing Dad made sense, but why did you drag my mother into things?' he asked.

'Necessity,' Alice replied. 'With your father dead, it was only a matter of time until she reported him missing. The police would have got themselves involved, and the last thing you needed was the authorities sniffing around, interfering in your business.'

'But by dragging her in, you knew what would happen. Anyway, surely you wanted her to report him missing. Don't you want the police to find you, to take you home, to reunite you with your family ... your *real* family?'

Alice glanced upwards, gazing at the roof as if mesmerised by something only she could see. Her silence indicated displeasure at the way the conversation was heading. For the first time, Hee Haw noticed a reluctance to talk about her own life.

The pair sat in silence, her gazing into space while he remained numb, overwhelmed by the way the day had panned out. After some time, he voiced a question which had been looping in his head.

'Why didn't you run?'

Alice broke her gaze and glanced at him, once more the knowing smile on her face.

'I don't understand what you're asking,' she said.

'When I killed my father, I was in here, kneeling by his body, trying to make sense of it, and you went outside, but you didn't run away. Why not?'

'Why would I run away?' Alice asked, surprised at the question.

'Well, for starters, I kidnapped you, and I'm going to do unspeakable things to you. Most people would've run when the opportunity arose.'

'But you're not going to do anything to me,' Alice said, her voice still heavy with innocence. 'I've been here with you for days, and you've not done anything bad to me. Well, not too bad.'

She grinned, displaying the space where her tooth was missing.

'I don't know,' Hee Haw muttered. 'I'm a monster. I mean, look around you. I killed my father and mother, didn't I?'

Alice giggled.

'I suppose so, but you won't hurt me.'

'I kidnapped you, and I wanted to rape and murder you,' Hee Haw said, surprised at how easy it was to admit his intentions. 'I punched you when you annoyed me, and I pulled some of your teeth out. I made you drink my piss. If I were you, I would have run when the chance came.'

'You didn't really kidnap me though, did you?'

Again, she flashed that knowing smile. As she did, the sensation of not being in control wormed its way under his skin.

It was true. The kidnapping had been too easy. He didn't so much snatch her, as she willingly followed him. After he crept up on her, she'd been friendly rather than surprised or afraid. She'd asked if he knew the way to the church, and he told her he did. Holding out his hand, she'd taken it without concern and allowed him to lead her away. She didn't once ask where they were going, nor did she question what was happening when they reached the shack. She'd been happy to go inside, to get in the box, to allow him to dominate her ... but had he ever been in control? Who was manipulating whom?

Even now, even after he'd slayed his mother and father, she was the one in control. She didn't fear him. If anything, she teased and taunted him, playing with his emotions like a cat with a mouse it's about to kill.

'This isn't over,' he hissed, desperate to regain the upper hand, but even he could hear the resignation in his own words. His father had been right. He never saw anything through to the end. When the going got tough, or when a challenge obstructed his path, he bailed out.

Alice smirked and slowly shook her head.

'You're right. It's not over. It'll never be over ... until it ends.'

'You're not making any sense,' Hee Haw huffed. 'If it'll never be over, it'll never end. Saying it'll never be over until it ends is like saying the day will last forever until it's night.'

'I am making sense,' Alice said, walking over to the box and climbing inside. 'In fact, I'm making perfect sense. I'm making so much sense it's almost nonsense. Now, don't you think you should tie me up in case I run away and tell someone you killed your parents?'

'What's the point?' Hee Haw asked with despondency. 'You didn't run away when you had the opportunity. You seem so fucking certain nothing bad will happen, that I'm not going to hurt you. Well, trust me, Alice: I'm still going to rape and murder you.'

'No, you're not,' Alice replied with a childlike giggle. 'You won't hurt me, ever, and do you know why?'

Hee Haw didn't respond.

'Do you know why?' Alice asked again, her words teasing.

'No,' Hee Haw muttered. 'Why don't you tell me, because you seem to know so much about me.'

'It's because you love me,' Alice said, squatting down in the crate. 'The first time you saw me, you fell in love with me. You didn't know it then, and to be fair, you might not have realised it yet, but you will. You love me and there's nothing you can do about it. Now, stop sulking and tie me up.'

'I don't love you,' Hee Haw snarled, dragging himself to his feet. 'I loathe you. I fucking detest you, and I *will* kill you. I'll hurt you more than you've ever been hurt. I'll make death a welcome relief for you.'

Inside the box, Alice giggled, a joyous snigger like a child playing hide-and-seek, but as Hee Haw approached it changed, becoming more of a twisted guffaw, a mocking howl of derision. Hesitating, he fought back the rage building inside him. She was taunting him, teasing like a bully, sneering at him as if he were nothing. She reminded him of his father, her scornful snorts of contempt like his when he sneered and scoffed.

Leaning against the crate, he brandished the machete.

'Shut up, you cunt, or I'll cut your tongue out.'

Alice poked out her tongue, wriggling it towards him, before she once more laughed, her face twisted in exaggerated hilarity.

'That's it,' Hee Haw snapped. 'You're pushing me too far.'

'You're pushing me too far,' Alice mimicked, her voice dramatically pathetic.

'I'm warning you,' he snarled, raising the machete.

Alice didn't flinch. Her eyes never left his as she stared deep into his being.

Holding the machete aloft in his trembling hand, he willed the blade to come down, to split her head in two, but his arm wouldn't move. Closing his eyes, he focused his effort into hacking her asunder, but every muscle and tendon in his body froze, as if he no longer had control of his limbs.

Why couldn't he kill her? He'd murdered his father and mother without hesitation. Chopping them into pieces had been simple, yet something wouldn't allow him to split Alice's head open. Was it because she was a child? Or was it because, as she claimed, he loved her?

Turning, he took a few strides to put distance between himself and the box. When he turned back, she sat up, leaning on the side of the crate, her elbows on the edge and hands under her chin as she watched him. She looked as if she was about to say something smart, something to undermine him.

'Don't make a fucking sound,' he snarled.

Alice theatrically clamped her mouth shut and, with one hand, mimicked locking her lips and throwing away the key. Even the way she looked at him displayed her utter contempt. She wasn't afraid. If anything, she was enjoying the confrontation, revelling in his discomfort.

Her words from earlier came back to him, haunting his thoughts. It'll never be over ... until it ends. Suddenly they did make sense. It would never be over, unless he ended it, unless he took action and stopped acting like a weak, pathetic cunt.

He'd show her, and he'd show his father, wherever he'd gone after his death. No doubt he'd be looking down, sneering as his son once more failed to see things through. Well, this time it would be different. This time, he'd take control.

It would be the perfect ending, the best way out. He'd kill Alice, then he'd take the three bodies into the house. After dousing the place with petrol, he'd set it alight. As the flames consumed the evidence, he'd run into the village, crying and wailing and pleading for help. He'd tell everyone his father had come home from town with a mysterious girl who he claimed was his daughter, and after a blazing row with his mother, had gone on the rampage, throwing petrol around and threatening to set their home on fire.

Who would doubt him? No one would suspect him of having killed the three of them before seeking help. It would be an end, and he'd walk away from the whole mess as a victim. They'd pity him, not accuse him.

As his grip on the machete handle tightened, Alice smirked and shook her head.

'They'll never fall for it,' she whispered. 'People will see right through you.'

Hee Haw froze. He hadn't spoken out loud, had he? How did she know what he was thinking? In that moment, he knew there was only one ending. Raising the machete, determined to strike, he inched towards her.

Alice sighed before speaking, her voice devoid of its usual innocent childishness.

'Give it up, *Colin*,' she said, almost spitting out his name. 'You haven't got the balls to see it through.'

'I'm not Colin,' he replied, speaking with confidence to reassure himself. 'I am Hee Haw.'

'It's too late, Colin,' she said coldly. 'That ship has sailed.'

'I'm not Colin,' he howled. 'I *am* Hee Haw.'

'No, you're not,' Alice said, her voice suddenly strong and determined.

'I am Hee Haw,' he bellowed, raising the machete.

'No, you're not,' Alice said, shaking her head, 'because I ... I am Hee Haw.'

11: UNTIL THE END

She laughed, the sound cruel and mocking. Colin rose on the balls of his feet, and using every last scrap of energy he could muster, swung the machete at Hee Haw's head. As the honed steel blade arced through the air towards its target, Hee Haw reached out, grasping the razor-sharp edge in her slender hand. The machete stopped with a sickening jolt as if it had hit an anvil, the vibration through the handle so intense Colin lost his grip as a burning pain shot up his arm.

Staggering backwards, he watched in terror as Hee Haw's mouth formed into a macabre grin, row upon row of blood-smeared, pointed teeth visible in her dark maw.

'Who the fuck do you think you are?' she growled, still holding the machete with a vice-like grip in her small, feminine hand. Despite the force with which she'd grabbed it, the blade hadn't drawn a single drop of blood.

'What gives you the audacity to challenge me?' she screamed. 'You're nothing but a loser, a ne'er-do-well, a mere nobody. How dare you confront me?'

Colin tried to back away but found himself pressed against the wall of the shack. Unable to retreat further, he watched as Hee Haw stepped from the box, her body glistening with a sheen reminiscent of a snake's skin. She no longer looked frail and malnourished. Her body was toned and lithe, like a wild animal.

'What was the point in your little charade, Colin?' she asked, her words barbed and cutting. 'Did you think by snatching me you'd find some sort of redemption? Did you believe you'd escape the fortress of self-loathing which you've built deep inside your head? Did you expect a road-to-fucking-Damascus moment, a revelation of some great truth, only attainable by brutalising a young child?'

As she approached, he couldn't move, his limbs exhausted and leaden as a creeping sense of dread washed over him.

'I don't know,' he whimpered. 'I really don't know.'

Shaking his head, he sobbed.

'You don't know?' Hee Haw asked with aggression, before cackling. 'It's a bit late to realise you don't fucking know, isn't it? It's a sorry state of affairs if you've come this far without thinking through what you hope to achieve. You snatch a young girl, threaten to rape her, to kill her, to ensure her last moments on this earth are as terrifying as you can, and you don't know what you hope to achieve?'

Colin shook his head.

'I'm sorry...' he blubbed.

'Sorry?' she shrieked. 'It's a bit late to be sorry. Don't you realise everything you do, every action you take, has repercussions? Did it never occur to you there would be a price you'd have to pay? This isn't a game. Do you understand me? Do I look like I'm playing a fucking game?'

Before he could respond, Hee Haw reached out her hand and, pushing two fingers into his nostrils, threw Colin's head back with force, cracking his skull off the wall. For a moment, the room whirled, and a surge of nausea hit him in the pit of his stomach. He wanted to fall, to slump to the floor, but for some reasons his trembling legs refused to buckle.

'I said, do I look like I'm playing a fucking game?'

As she snarled in his face, Colin smelled her breath. It stank of brimstone and burning flesh, of death and decay and desolation, of shame and self-loathing. It stank of Hell. It stank of Hee Haw.

'No,' he half-sobbed.

'No what?' Hee Haw barked.

'No, it doesn't look like you're playing a game,' he whimpered, his words dying away into a fragile whisper as he finished his sentence.

Hee Haw reached out her hand, but instead of striking him, she stroked his hair, gently, like a mother comforting a little child.

'Do you remember, Colin?' she cooed, her voice once again soft and innocent. 'Do you remember what I told you?'

Colin stood, trembling, wracking his brains. What did she mean? She'd said so many things. Which one was she referring to? Uncertain what to say, he made a guess.

'Was it when you said this wasn't a game?'

Hee Haw sighed and whispered, 'I'm disappointed in you, Colin.'

As she did, he realised her breath had changed. It smelled of the forest on a frosty morning, earthy and floral and rich with pine resin. It was momentarily intoxicating, soothing, but then a spike of terror overwhelmed the comfortable feeling.

Shaking with fear, he tried to dredge up a memory, to find the answer she sought.

'Was it ... I don't know ... when you said I was in love with you?'

She laughed, a pitying chortle which made him feel small and insignificant.

'All I wanted was love, Colin,' she whispered. 'It was what I needed, but instead you gave me spite and malice.'

'I could love you,' he whimpered. 'I could, if it were what you wanted.'

'No, you couldn't,' she said coldly.

He stood, trembling, his head spinning, but much as he tried, he couldn't remember anything she'd told him which might be significant.

She started to hum, a melodic tune which immediately sent an unpleasant, electric shiver through his body. It was the little song she'd sung on the night she'd bitten him. As she hummed, he could hear the words echoing in his head.

'Hark! Hark! The dogs do bark,
'The beggars have come to town.
'Some in rags, and some in tags,
'And one in a white silk gown.'

Tears bubbled up under his eyelids, and despite his best efforts, he couldn't prevent them from tumbling down his cheeks. Feeling the wet tracks on his face, sorrow erupted from his core, a wave of utter desolation sweeping over him.

Hee Haw stopped humming and asked, 'Can you remember yet, that thing I told you?'

Colin shook his head as fresh rivulets of tears streaked his face.

'Do you want a clue?' she asked in a sing-song voice, teasing him.

Colin nodded.

'I said it'll never be over...'

'Until it ends,' he sobbed.

'Well, now it ends,' she said with finality.

Taking a step back, Hee Haw let go of the machete blade, flicking it up in the air. As it reached the peak of its travel, she grabbed the handle with the skill of an executioner.

Colin closed his eyes, bowed his head, and awaited the inevitable ending.

If you have enjoyed this book, please consider leaving a review at Amazon, Goodreads or Godless.com.

Thank you.

ABOUT THE AUTHOR

Peter Caffrey creates stories stained with the darkest of dark humour, featuring elements of splattery filth, horror, bizarro and absurdity.

Alongside numerous books, his work has also appeared in a number of anthologies including ABC's of Terror (Vol 4), Call Me Hoop, Unamerican Trash, In Uterus, Prose in Poor Taste (Vol 2), The Best of Bizarro Fiction (Vol 2) and The Bumper Book of British Bizarro. He has also featured in many publications including Underbelly, Horror Sleaze Trash, Infernal Ink, Terror House, Frontier Tales and Schlock!

He likes apes, dislikes gravity, and is unlikely to change.

petercaffrey.com

The God of Wanking

After accidentally reviving a dormant demon, Diego is offered the deal of a lifetime. He can have his way with any woman he wishes, fulfilling his carnal desires. All he has to do in return is provide a regular supply of sperm. Like most schoolboys, he's in the habit of regularly wanking, so he figures he has nothing to lose by agreeing to the pact.

Once the demon takes control, he manipulates the situation, leaving Diego trapped in a waking nightmare. The daily duty becomes a millstone, dragging him into an abyss of masturbatory misery.

Why does the demon want his semen, and has it anything to do with the numerous elderly women who are falling pregnant and giving birth to devil babies with unfeasibly large cocks? With the clergy and their militia hunting down the source of the impregnations, Diego finds himself a victim of the chaos.

As his world crumbles, the only hope is to free himself from the pact.

'An excellently-paced, splatteriffic encounter with an trickster god, full of sodomy, corncob cocks, and evil bastards.'
Regina Watts

'If Caffrey doesn't ascend to bizzaro/horror cult status I'm giving up wanking for good.'
Simon McHardy

'So glad I read this book. Made me as happy as the day I discovered cock rings existed.'
Sean Hawker

Dog Food

Trapped between normality and insanity, somewhere in the darkness, exists a state of consciousness so bleak, so miserable, so inescapable, that it can erode the very fabric of a man's will to survive.

David Miller hates coming home from holidays. The return journey is always stressful. When his break in the Algarve ends, the journey home is plagued by his miserable wife and squealing children, while the irritations of budget airlines push him to the edge.

But once the plane lands, things get darker when he meets the bald man.

Dog Food is an absurdist tale of one man's descent into the abyss...

Reviews from Goodreads

"A disturbing read that instills a sense of creeping dread. Peter Caffrey is the mad genius of indie horror."

"An awesomely, enjoyable, creepy, mind twisting story!"

"Funny, frightening, surreal and speckled with grossness."

"What an absolute orgy of mind-fucks!"

"Five stars. This is a 'Twilight Zone' style tale with an ending open for interpretation."

"This story is well written, intriguing, incredible, bizarre and absurd. It made me question myself all along. It was mind blowing."

Fucked-Up Bedtime Stories (Series One)

Ten year old Arnold has a cuddly friend, Jimmy the Chimp. His toy ape is his companion, his fellow adventurer and his advisor. No one else can hear Jimmy when he talks, and there's nothing about modern life the chimp doesn't know. Escaping from the world of Mummy and Daddy, the pair set out to have a series of adventures, aided by the fact Jimmy the Chimp is a Satanic necromancer.

Let their enchanting escapades relax and amuse you as you slip into a slumber filled with the sweetest of sweet dreams.

This collection includes all twelve stories from the first series.

Goodreads Reviews

"Well written, gross, vile, depraved and original."

"The humor is outrageous and laugh out loud, and mixes well with the violence that will make a veteran extreme horror reader cringe."

"Shocking, disturbing, gross, horrible, vile ... but absolutely brilliant!"

"I can't believe Peter Caffrey took things this far!"

"This is one of my all-time favorite series, and they just keep getting better and better."

"Haven't laughed so much since my mother-in-law fell down the stairs and broke her leg."

The Butcher's Other Daughter

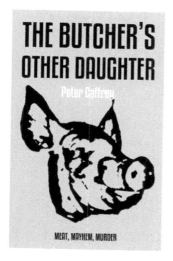

Jacques Dupont is a pork butcher in the small town of Sainte-Marie-sur-Ariège. On the surface, he appears to be an unremarkable man, but Jacques has a secret, a previous life he is desperate to ensure remains forgotten.

When the two worlds collide, the outcome is cataclysmic, throwing his life into a maelstrom of violence and rage which threatens to overwhelm everything he holds dear.

If you like your splatterpunk laced with a smattering of charcuterie, then Sainte-Marie-sur-Ariège may be the town for you!

The Butcher's Other Daughter is a tale of meat, mayhem and murder.

Goodreads Reviews

"Excellent writing! I loved this one. Revenge with a twist and pork treats."

"This was a dark twisted little revenge story that, once I started, I had to finish. Peter Caffrey creates awesome characters, and I like how the book went back and forth, telling the story though each of the characters' point of view. Plus there are recipes at the end, so you can make your own tasty meat treats, which is totally awesome."

"Oohhh, this one was darker than the others I've read by Peter Caffrey. It reminded me a little of Sweeney Todd. Once I started reading this one I had to keep going."

Whores Versus Sex Robots (and Other Sordid Tales of Erotic Automatons)

When the introduction of brothels manned by AI-powered sex robots threaten the profitability of the world's oldest profession, the street girls decide it's time to fight for their future and bring the punters back where they belong: between their legs.

Hatching a drastic plan to ensure the Johns turn against erotic automatons, the whores take on the brave new world, but inadvertently unleash a battle for survival as technology's finest refuse to take the challenge lying down.

Whores versus Sex Robots is a seedy, science fiction, splatterpunk, tongue-in-cheek novella. The book also includes a selection of other stories addressing the rise of the sex robots.

WARNING: Despite the title, this book is NOT erotica, and is totally unsuitable for masturbatory purposes – unless, of course, you like to knock yourself out while reading about the violence and pain of modern society, the frailty of the human condition, the abandonment of hope, and the depths of selfishness to which mankind can (and often will) sink. If that's the case, then buy this book and wank yourself silly. Otherwise, please do not interfere with your sexual apparatus while reading these stories.

The Devil's Hairball

When Victor Holycross commits an act of heinous sacrilege at the Festival of the Blessed Virgin, he unwittingly instigates a curse which transforms his wife and daughter into the Devil's hairballs. To seek absolution for his sin and to lift the hairy plague from his family, a penance is given: the recovery of stolen religious relics. Under pressure from a less-than-Godly Cardinal and his malicious henchman, Victor has little choice but to accept his fate.

With a time frame of 40 days and 40 nights and a decrepit bicycle as his sole form of transport, he finds himself helped (and, more often than not, hindered) by a one-legged whore, a talking dog with strange sexual proclivities, and an attack-nun.

As Victor is thrust into a maelstrom of demonic confrontations, unholy alliances and duplicitous relationships, he soon discovers that the world is a far darker place than he ever anticipated.

"If Dante's Inferno, The Wizard of Oz, and Monty Python's Life of Brian had a sacrilegious threesome it may look quite a bit like The Devil's Hairball. It's wonderfully absurd, a bit whimsical, and completely bizarre."
Biblioculus.com

"One of the most bizarre story ideas I have come across in recent years."
Jim Mcleod – Gingernuts of Horror

"Improper. That's how to sum up Peter Caffrey's raucous horror/comedy The Devil's Hairball ... dirty humour drips from every page."
Kendall Reviews

The Crucifiction of Bastard Jesus

"The book which made the Pope's sphincter tighten and his testes retract into his body."

The story of Easter is well known, but the church is more tight-lipped about the second son of God who was created as a back-up plan to the more notorious Jesus Christ. While the birth of the Plan B messiah should have been terminated once the first-choice conception went ahead, an administrative cock-up in heaven resulted in the boy being born in Bethlehem, close to a somewhat more infamous stable.

The two sons of God lived separate lives. Despite this, in a cruel irony, the second son of God was also crucified on Good Friday, much like his more famous sibling, but in vastly different circumstances.

Peter Caffrey and Lindsay Crook, who happen to be theological historians as well as writers of filthy tales, join forces to reveal the harrowing story of the man referred to by the Vatican, in its most secret records, as Bastard Jesus.

Goodreads Reviews

"The Crucifiction of Bastard Jesus is hilarious! This well written, irreverent and disgusting book made me laugh out loud."

"Funny as fuck! I caught myself laughing out loud several times."

"This book is comedy gold. I highly recommend it."

Cock-A-Voodoo-Doo (And Other Twisted Love Stories)

Cock-A-Voodoo-Doo and Other Twisted Love Stories is a collection of three novelettes: Cock-A-Voodoo-Doo, Dolls' House Diabolic, and The Perils of Dating Celine.

Cock-A-Voodoo-Doo

Based on a true story which took place during 1970, never discussed after the sorry shambles unfolded, and only referred to by the family as 'the Christmas incident', the events of that time had a profound impact on a young and innocent boy.

No names have been changed, because there are no innocent parties.

Dolls' House Diabolic

Dave loved Susan. He really loved Susan. Nothing made him happier than when she agreed to marry him. As he set off to Bangkok for his stag party, he promised her one thing: he'd avoid the go-go bars. However, when the other stags insisted on visiting a pussy show, Dave ended up being dragged to the Dolls' House.

Dolls' House Diabolic is the story of one man's battle with the biggest demons: his own guilt and shame. Will Dave and Susan live happily ever after, or will one random act condemn their future?

The Perils of Dating Celine

After watching a TV Chef's hour-long special on all things pasta, the urge to purchase a pasta machine becomes all encompassing for Terry. Tracking down a second-hand one on-line, he makes the purchase, and when the machine arrives it includes a note from the mysterious Celine.The Perils of Dating Celine is a glimpse into what could happen if people simply followed their hearts.

Like a Tramp Yelling at Trains (And Other Unpoetic Noises)

When I was a boy, there was a tramp who lived in a derelict factory near our house. On the way to school, we'd often see him, standing at the side of the road by the railway lines, staring at the spot where the train tunnel ended and the tracks emerged into the outside world. As the trains thundered from the darkness into the morning light, he'd launch into a tirade of nonsensical babble, shouting curses and abominations.

I understood him. Not his words, not his shouts and curses, but his purpose. I too shared a need to expunge the detritus which built up in my head. I required a cathartic expulsion of the madness and chaos which festered in my thoughts.

This collection is just that: a medley of insane and inane shouts and screams, a collage of verbal ticks, a cornucopia of inky doodlings. Some are random ideas which sneak into my brain, others are heart-felt and personal reflections, and a few are just humorous cul-de-sacs. Some are the germs from which stories or novels have grown, but most went no further than the form in which they are replicated in this dosshouse of words.

A few of you might find something which amuses, and others won't. Whichever group you fall into, I want to thank you, because you are my train, thundering out from the darkness of the tunnel, and I'm just a random pissy old tramp, screaming abuse at you.

Freak Fuck

Freak Fuck is the eighth book in the *Fucking Scumbags Burn In Hell* series from Godless.

Doctor Fairweather, a disgraced cosmetic surgeon, is a dedicated fan of easy money. Running sham clinics, he preys on the vane and those seeking another shot at youth. But Fairweather desires one thing more than easy money: a beautiful woman whose perfection he can violate and destroy, creating a hideous monster for his own gratification.

When a series of unforseen events results in a chance encounter with Nurse Hooper, the doctor wonders if he has finally found the right host to allow him to create his ultimate freak fuck.

Goodreads Reviews

"This was the first time I've read Caffrey and I loved his style of writing. The descriptions made me feel like I was there, and were gruesome and brutal without being overdone. It was just right."

"Damn, this one was brilliantly creative and wildly brutal."

"As usual, Caffrey didn't disappoint with his tale of one messed-up plastic surgeon. Gross, demented and humorous, this story was fun to read."

"Freak Fuck is quite the little nasty. Like most anything Peter Caffrey writes, there are elements of extreme horror, bizarro, comedy, and revenge."

Nympho Nurses' Ton-Up Terror
(Mondo Perverso #1)

When the nurses from St Hilda's Hospital set off on their annual motorcycle run, the last thing they expect is to be caught up in the fallout of a chemical weapon debacle, but that's exactly what happens.

Join Fanny Batter, Ginger Bush and Dawn Double-Dee as they battle against the sex plague and a horde of twisted deformos, while also enjoying some high-octane thrills and spills.

This is your only chance to enjoy one of Terry Funicular's pivotal works now that the Mondo Perverso films have been consigned to the flames of history, so dive right in; the water's fucking filthy!

Nympho Nurses' Ton-Up Terror is part of the 'Mondo Perverso Night Out at the Cinema Without Going to the Cinema but with a Similar Feeling Albeit in a Book Experience' series, and is supplied with a free-of-charge audio file which not only includes the full narration, but also has everything to create a fleapit cinema mood, from incidental music, trailers, a message from the director, an intermission and adverts. To enjoy the full immersive experience, it is recommended that you do listen to the audio file. Really. It's worth it.

Exclusive to Godless.com

Zombie Cheerleaders on LSD (Mondo Perverso #2)

When the archaeological society of Beavertown High School go on a dig, they discover their campsite is next to the Gallstonebury Festival at Turdy Farm. After Glenda Gash is bitten by a rat at the dig site, falls ill and dies, some dropouts from the festival plan to feed the girls LSD with the intention of sexually abusing them, but when Glenda reappears, their world is torn apart.

As Zed Leppelin hit the stage, the cheerleaders fight back with everything they've got!

This is your only chance to enjoy one of Terry Funicular's pivotal works now that the Mondo Perverso films have been consigned to the flames of history, so dive right in; the water's fucking filthy!

Zombie Cheerleaders on LSD is part of the '**Mondo Perverso Night Out at the Cinema Without Going to the Cinema but with a Similar Feeling Albeit in a Book Experience**' series, and is supplied with a free-of-charge audio file which not only includes the full narration, but also has everything to create a fleapit cinema mood, from incidental music, trailers, a message from the director, an intermission and adverts. To enjoy the full immersive experience, it is recommended that you do listen to the audio file. Really. It's worth it.

Exclusive to Godless.com

Star Whores: Return of the Dildo (Mondo Perverso #3)

When the Holy Order of Star Whores are arrested in Galaxy NGC-1300, the authorities confiscate all their assets as they're classified as being gained via immoral earnings. Included amongst the seized items is an entity, a God, the Lord Dildo.

In order to rescue the deity, the Star Whores turn to space pirate Buzz Lovebeads who, along with his sidekicks Hands Solo and Easy Leia, goes in search of the entity ... despite being chased by the evil lawman Garth Gayder who is intent on capturing the pirates.

This is your only chance to enjoy one of Terry Funicular's pivotal works now that the Mondo Perverso films have been consigned to the flames of history, so dive right in; the water's fucking filthy!

Star Whores: Return of the Dildo is part of the 'Mondo Perverso Night Out at the Cinema Without Going to the Cinema but with a Similar Feeling Albeit in a Book Experience' series, and is supplied with a free-of-charge audio file which not only includes the full narration, but also has everything to create a fleapit cinema mood, from incidental music, trailers, a message from the director, an intermission and adverts. To enjoy the full immersive experience, it is recommended that you do listen to the audio file. Really. It's worth it.

Exclusive to Godless.com

Girl Gang Clusterfuck in Cell Block B (Mondo Perverso #4)

When prison warder Molly McGinty checks in for her night shift on Friday the 13th, little does she know the horrors which lie ahead. While the numerous girl gangs tool up for an all-out war over drugs, tobacco and toilet wine, Molly wants nothing more than a quiet shift.

She has a lot to think about, not least her love for Prisoner 117213, also known as Big Bertha. When the carnage erupts, she faces a choice: does she follow duty or love? Which of her emotions will be stronger: her fanatical devotion to the law, or the throbbing feeling in her vagina?

It's all kicking off in Cell Block B, where the violence is hard and the women are moist.

Girl Gang Clusterfuck in Cell Block B is part of the 'Mondo Perverso Night Out at the Cinema Without Going to the Cinema but with a Similar Feeling Albeit in a Book Experience' series, and is supplied with a free-of-charge audio file which not only includes the full narration, but also has everything to create a fleapit cinema mood, from incidental music, trailers, a message from the director, an intermission and adverts. To enjoy the full immersive experience, it is recommended that you do listen to the audio file. Really. It's worth it.

Exclusive to Godless.com

Cannibal She-Devils of the Umpopo Delta (Mondo Perverso #5)

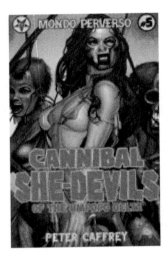

Travelling along the Umpopo river, the missionaries of Saint Xavier's are eager to spread the word of the Lord to the local savage tribes. However, their fate takes a turn of the worse when they meet Queen Bazoomas and her warrior women. Captured, abused, tortured, and pegged with hand-carved tribal dildos, they soon realise the Umpopo Delta is no place for God-fearing men.

As the cannibal she-devils exhibit their taste for man-meat, the missionaries realise their only chance of survival is to submit to the will of their captors and become the sexual playthings of the wild warrior women.

Cannibal She-Devils of the Umpopo Delta is part of the '**Mondo Perverso Night Out at the Cinema Without Going to the Cinema but with a Similar Feeling Albeit in a Book Experience**' series, and is supplied with a free-of-charge audio file which not only includes the full narration, but also has everything to create a fleapit cinema mood, from incidental music, trailers, a message from the director, an intermission and adverts. To enjoy the full immersive experience, it is recommended that you do listen to the audio file. Really. It's worth it.

Exclusive to Godless.com

Wino Women's Car Park Catfight
(Mondo Perverso #6)

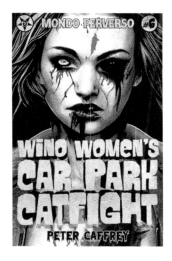

When the wino women start a turf war in the local multi-storey car park, things quickly turn violent as the boozy hags battle the pissed-up slags. Despite attempts by Walter, the Car Park Warden, to restore law and order, the situation turns into a right royal shit-show when a car owned by sleaze baron Charlie Lovespuds is broken into.

Finding what they believe to be imported booze, the women go on an epic binge, unaware they're downing bottle after bottle of an illicit aphrodisiac love drug he has smuggled into the country from Cambodia. Charlie wants payment or his drugs back, Walter wants his car-park free of winos, and the women want a good seeing to.

Wino Women's Car Park Catfight is part of the '**Mondo Perverso Night Out at the Cinema Without Going to the Cinema but with a Similar Feeling Albeit in a Book Experience**' series, and is supplied with a free-of-charge audio file which not only includes the full narration, but also has everything to create a fleapit cinema mood, from incidental music, trailers, a message from the director, an intermission and adverts. To enjoy the full immersive experience, it is recommended that you do listen to the audio file. Really. It's worth it.

Exclusive to Godless.com

Printed in Great Britain
by Amazon